Anonymous

The River St. Lawrence

Anonymous

The River St. Lawrence

Reprint of the original, first published in 1859.

1st Edition 2022 | ISBN: 978-3-37512-170-9

Verlag (Publisher): Salzwasser Verlag GmbH, Zeilweg 44, 60439 Frankfurt, Deutschland
Vertretungsberechtigt (Authorized to represent): E. Roepke, Zeilweg 44, 60439 Frankfurt, Deutschland
Druck (Print): Books on Demand GmbH, In de Tarpen 42, 22848 Norderstedt, Deutschland

THE

RIVER ST. LAWRENCE,

IN ONE PANORAMIC VIEW,

From Niagara Falls to Quebec,

TOGETHER WITH DESCRIPTIONS AND ILLUSTRATIONS OF

THE THOUSAND ISLANDS, CITIES IN CANADA,

LAKES, RAPIDS, RIVERS, AND FALLS, AND OTHER OBJECTS AND
PLACES OF INTEREST.

WITH NUMEROUS ENGRAVINGS.

NEW YORK:
ALEX. HARTHILL, 20 NORTH WILLIAM STREET.
ROSS & TOUSEY; H. DEXTER & CO.; HENDRICKSON, BLAKE & LONG.
TORONTO:—McLEAR & CO. MONTREAL:—B. DAWSON & SON.
And Sold by all Booksellers and Newsmen.

PANORAMA

OF THE

RIVER ST. LAWRENCE,

FROM

NIAGARA FALLS TO QUEBEC.

CONTENTS.

LIST OF ILLUSTRATIONS.

TRIP DOWN THE ST. LAWRENCE.

Via the Lakes and Rapids.

Whilst other tours, in different parts of the United States and Canada, have their attractions — particularly, by railroad — and severally present sufficient inducements for a visit from the tourist; none, we believe, presents so great a variety of scenery—and that of the finest character, accompanied by comfortable locomotion and a few exciting incidents on the way—as are to be met with on the trip from Niagara to Montreal and Quebec *via* Lake Ontario—down the Rapids of the noble St. Lawrence—through the Thousand Islands, and the various other lakes, canals, etc., on the route.

This route may be taken either by steamer all the way from Lewiston or Niagara, or from there to Toronto, Kingston, Cape Vincent, or any of the other points of stoppage on the river hereafter stated; after visiting which, the tourist can embark on board the steamer again at any of the stopping places, and proceed on his journey.

To render this trip as intelligible as possible, we propose placing the names of each place of interest, on both sides of the river, in such order that the stranger will at once be able to know on which side each town is situated. This will be seen at once by making a division in the page, representing the channel of the river, with the towns, rapids, lakes and canals placed in their relative positions; so that, with the distances and routes given elsewhere, we hope to render such information as will be useful and interesting to the reader. We shall take LEWISTON as the starting point.

ROUTE FROM LEWISTON (NIAGARA) TO QUEBEC.

TOWNS AND STOPPING-PLACES.

CANADIAN, OR NORTH BANK OF RIVER.	AMERICAN, OR SOUTH BANK OF RIVER.
QUEENSTOWN, a village situated nearly opposite to Lewiston. Its chief objects of attraction are the handsome Suspension Bridge, with Brock's Monument, situated on the heights, from which a most magnificent view of the lake and the surrounding country is obtained.	LEWISTON is the point from which the steamer starts—being at the head of river navigation—about 7 miles from Niagara Falls, and 7 miles from the mouth of the river, whence it falls into the lake. The Buffalo, Niagara Falls and Lewiston Railroad terminates at this place.

LAKE ONTARIO.

This is the smallest and most easterly of the five great lakes which communicate with the St. Lawrence, and divides the State of New York from Canada, on the north. It is 190 miles long, and its greatest breadth 55 miles. Its greatest depth is 600 feet, and it is navigable in every part for the largest-sized ships. It is never entirely closed with ice, and rarely freezes, even in the coldest weather, except in shallow places along the shore. In summer time, a sail upon this lake is delightful, especially to the angler, who, if he chooses to cast his lines into its usually placid waters, will find no dearth of fish, which abound here in great variety. On either side of the lake are seen numerous towns and villages, several of which are of considerable business importance. We append brief notices of the most noted of these places.

CANADIAN SIDE.	AMERICAN SIDE.
In proceeding along the north, or Canadian, side of the lake, the first point touched is	The first stopping-place on the American, or south, side of the Lake is YOUNGSTOWN, 6 miles below, and 1 mile

21

Toronto, the second most important city in Canada. This city presents a much finer appearance from the lake than when approached by railway. Toronto boasts of a large number of fine buildings and elegant churches, as well as of extensive and tasteful blocks of business stores; and the beauty of their appearance is much enhanced by the large number of trees, and the quantity of shrubbery that adorns many of its streets. King street, its principal thoroughfare, is two miles long, and is lined on both sides with handsome stores and public buildings.

Leaving Toronto, the first town of any particular note, on the Canadian side, is

Port Whitby, 29 miles below. This is the chief town in Ontario County, and contains near 4,000 inhabitants. It is a station on the Grand Trunk Railway, and is a stopping-place for steamers from Toronto to Rochester, etc.

Oshawa, 4 miles below, is a fine town of 3,000 inhabitants, on the Grand Trunk Railroad, and communicating with the interior towns by lines of stages. A great quantity of flour is shipped from here.

Bowmanville, 10 miles below, lies a little back of the lake, to which it is connected by *Darlington Harbour*. In 1850, the place was incorporated a village, since which period its growth has been very rapid. The town has excellent water power within and around it. The country around is unsurpassed for fertility and salubrity by any in Canada. It has a population of about 5,000.

Port Hope is about 20 miles below Bowmanville, and, like it, is a station on the Grand Trunk Railroad. It is also connected by railway with Lindsay, 40 miles, and with Peterborough, 29 miles distant. Steamers also ply between this place and several towns lying north, on Lake Sturgeon. Port Hope is built on an acclivity, the summit of which is capped with beach and pine, and clothed with villas, embowered among the trees. The principal street runs from the harbour to the top of the hill, and is lined with elegant stores, beautiful dwellings and commodious hotels. The Town Hall and Montreal Bank form prominent objects to a spectator placed upon the quay. And the graceful

above, old Fort Niagara, at the mouth of the river, and which possesses a fine natural harbour, open at all seasons of the year. The river is here about half a mile in width, across which a ferry plies to the village of Niagara, on the Canadian side.

Fort Niagara.—In passing into the lake, this old relic of former times is especially noticeable. As early as 1679, this spot was inclosed by La Salle, the explorer of the Mississippi. In 1725, a pallisade fort was constructed by the French. In 1759, it was taken by the British, who, in 1796, gave it into the hands of the Americans. In 1813, it was taken again by the British, and recaptured by the Americans in 1815. There is no doubt that the dungeons of this old fort have been the scenes of horrible suffering and of crime, from the times of the old Indian and French wars, up to the days of the Revolution. In its close and impregnable dungeons, the light of day never shone; and here, doubtless, many a poor prisoner has been compelled to undergo the "torture," in addition to his other nameless sufferings.

As, after entering the lake, no place of much importance is reached for some hours, the tourist should embrace this opportunity of getting a good view of the scenes he is about leaving. On a clear day, a fine view is presented of Brock's Monument, and the grand heights of Queenstown, 9 or 10 miles distant, which rise nearly 500 feet above the waters of the lake.

After passing several small settlements, we reach

Charlotte, or Port Genesee, at the mouth of the River Genesee, port of entry for Rochester, 7 miles distant, and 87 miles from Niagara. This town possesses a safe harbour, being protected by two long piers, on one of which is located a lighthouse. A number of steamers run daily from here to several of the principal places on both sides of the lake.

The Falls of Genesee.—These beautiful falls, second only to Niagara, are objects worthy of notice. The banks of the Genesee, just above Charlotte, rise from 50 to 150 feet in height. The river is navigable as far as Carthage, which may be called a suburb of Rochester. From this curve of the viaduct, resting on piers of solid masonry, over which the Grand Trunk Railway is carried, tends to enhance the picturesqueness of the view. The town is surrounded by a rich agricultural district, diversified by hill and dale, wood and stream; the evidence of which is the number of wagons—crammed with quarters of fat beef, mutton and pork, turkeys, chickens, eggs butter, vegetables and fish—to be seen crowding the Town Hall Square on Saturdays.

The lumber trade carried on at this port is also very extensive. Population about 8,000.

Cobura, 8 miles below Port Hope, is the terminus of the Coburg and Peterborough Railroad. It has a good harbour, and does an extensive shipping business with Rochester, and other cities on the opposite side of the lake. Victoria College, established by act of the Provincial Legislature, in 1842, is in this town. It also contains the most extensive cloth manufactories in the Province. There are also iron, marble and leather manufactories, with a number of breweries and distilleries, 9 good hotels, and 60 or 70 substantial stores. Population about 6,000.

COLBORNE, 14 miles below Coburg, is a flourishing town, having a fine back country, whose produce finds quick sales in its markets. It has a good landing for steamers, many of which touch here on their passages up and down the lake.

A good business is done in this town in curing white-fish and salmon-trout, which abound in the lake, and are taken in great quantities. A stage-route is established between this place and Norwood, 32 miles distance. Fare, $2.

Leaving Colborne, the steamer soon reaches the widest part of the lake, and, running a distance of some 25 miles, passes *Nicholas Point* and *Island, Wicked Point*, and *Point Peter*, on the latter of which is a fine light-house. This light is a conspicuous object to mariners, who, when off Prince Edward's, the main-land, experience the full force of easterly and westerly winds.

DUCK ISLAND, which is attached to Canada, is another noted object for the mariner, either ascending or descending the

place, to Rochester proper, there are a succession of falls and rapids, some of the former being very grand and imposing. The falls at Carthage are 75 feet, one a little further up is 20 feet, and the great falls—within the city, a few feet from the Central Railroad Bridge—is 96 feet. It was at these latter falls that the once famous Sam Patch made his last leap, by which he lost his life. He commenced his singular career by plunging from the Pawtucket Falls, in Rhode Island, and afterwards continued to jump from all the high bridges, and other elevated points in the country, including Niagara, without meeting an accident. It is supposed that he was intoxicated at the time he made his last jump, and hence lost his balance during his descent, and struck the water horizontally, which must have knocked the breath entirely out of his body, as he was not seen to rise after striking the water, although 10,000 spectators were anxiously looking for his appearance. His dead body was found some miles below the falls.

Further up the river, near the town of Portage, N. Y., there are three beautiful falls, respectively, 60, 90 and 110 feet, all within the space of 2 miles, each differing in character, and each having peculiar attractions. But more wonderful, than the falls, are the stupendous walls of the river, which rise almost perpendicularly, to a height of 400 feet, and extend along the stream, for 3 miles, with almost as much regularity and symmetry as if constructed by art.

Leaving the mouth of the Genesee, the steamer passes the small town of *Pultneyville*, and some other lesser settlements, and reaches the mouth of

GREAT SODUS BAY, which is 5 miles long and 3 miles in breadth, and makes an excellent, safe harbour, the entrance of which is protected by substantial piers, built by the United States.

SODUS POINT is a small town, and port of entry, situated at the mouth of Sodus Bay.

LITTLE SODUS BAY, 14 miles below Great Sodus, is another good anchorage ground, for vessels to ride, in times of severe weather.

OSWEGO is on both sides of Oswego

lake, as it is the first important island met, in the passage from the head of the lake, on the Canada side. In former years, immense quantities of wild ducks gathered upon this island, and hence its name.

AMHERST ISLAND, also belonging to Canada, lies a little further on. It is a large body of very fertile land, which is under a good state of cultivation. Beyond this island, we come to the end of the lake, and soon enter the mouth of the St. Lawrence River. We now pass two islands— *Gage* and *Wolf*—which are the first of that astonishing group known as the " Thousand Islands." We next come to KINGSTON, which is probably the finest-looking city in Canada, although not doing a business equal to Montreal or Toronto. A tourist, speaking of this city, says:

" The view of the city and surrounding scenery is not surpassed by the approaches to any other city in America. A few miles above Kingston, the waters of Lake Ontario are divided by the first of the long series of islands so well known to tourists as the ' Thousand Islands,' of which Simcoe and Grand, or Wolfe Islands, opposite the city, may be looked upon as strongholds designed by nature to withstand the encroaches of the waves of Ontario. On approaching from the west, by water, the first object that attracts the traveller's attention is *Fort Henry*, with the naval station of *Fort Frederick* at its base, and its attendant battlements, fortifications, towers and redoubts."

FORT HENRY is a favourite resort for visitors, and its elevated position affords the best view that can be had of the city, lake and surrounding country.

The principal public buildings are the City Hall, Court-House, Roman Catholic Cathedral, Queen's College, Roman Catholic College, General Hospital, Penitentiary, 16 or 18 fine churches, banking-houses, etc. The City Hall is one of the finest edifices in Canada, built of cut limestone, at an expense of near $100,000. It has a spacious hall, holding over 1,000 persons. There are 20 steamers, and about 50 sailing vessels, owned here; and these, besides other Canadian and American craft, are mostly occupied in

River, at its entrance into Lake Ontario and is the largest and most active city on the lake. There are from 15 to 20 flouring-mills, making over 10,000 barrels of flour per day when in operation, and about a dozen elevators, with storage-room for 2,000,000 bushels of grain. It is handsomely built, with streets 100 feet wide, crossing each other at right angles. The river divides the city into nearly two equal parts, which are connected by two bridges, above ship navigation.

The number of vessels which arrive and depart from this port is very large. It is estimated that one-half of the entire trade of Canada with the United States is carried on with Oswego. A railroad, 36 miles in length, connects Oswego with Syracuse. The Oswego Canal also connects at Syracuse with the Erie Canal. Oswego ranks as one of the greatest grain markets in the world, being second on this continent only to Chicago. From her position, she must continue to hold her advantage, and, in spite of all rivalry, will always command the greatest portion of Canadian trade. The population of Oswego is about 20,000.

Leaving Oswego, we pass *Mexico Bay*, into which empties

SALMON RIVER, at the mouth of which is a small town, called *Port Ontario*. *Salmon River Falls* are classed among the greatest natural curiosities of the country. The current of the river is disturbed, about 6 miles from its mouth, by 2 miles of rapids, which terminate in a fall of 107 feet. At high water, the sheet is 250 feet in width, but, at low water, is narrowed to about half that extent. At the foot of the falls the water is very deep, and abounds in fine fish, such as salmon, trout and bass.

SACKETT's HARBOUR, 45 miles north of Oswego, possesses one of the most secure harbours on the lake. During the war of 1812, with England, it was used as the rendezvous of the American fleet on Lake Ontario. A large war-vessel, commenced at that time, still remains here under cover. Madison Barracks, garrisoned by United States troops, is situated near the landing.

BLACK RIVER, just beyond, is 120 miles long, but its navigation is much impeded by a succession of rapids and falls. It

24

carrying passengers and produce which come from inland by the Rideau Canal, and from the Bay of Quinte, to the different ports on the lake.

There are several mineral springs in Kingston, which have attained some celebrity for their medical properties. One of these, situated near the Penitentiary, is said to resemble the celebrated Cheltenham Springs, in England. Another, whose waters are unusually strong, and, by analyzation, have been found to contain valuable medical virtues, has been likened to the Artesian Well at St. Catherine's.

gives, however, great water power, and its banks are covered with prosperous towns and villages.

CHAUMONT BAY, just above Black River, abounds in a variety of fine fish, large quantities of which are taken by established fisheries.

CAPE ST. VINCENT is nearly opposite Grand or Wolf Island, and is the northern terminus of the Watertown and Rome Railroad. In the warm months, this place is much resorted to by fishing and pleasure parties, being contiguous to the "Thousand Islands."

THE THOUSAND ISLANDS.

THESE Islands, which have obtained a world-wide celebrity, consist of fully 1800 islands, of all sizes and shapes—from a few yards long, to several miles in length; some, presenting little or nothing but bare masses of rock, whilst others are so thickly wooded over, that nothing but the most gorgeous green foliage (in summer) is to be seen; whilst, in autumn, the leaves present colours of different hues of light crimson, yellow, purple and other colours scarcely imaginable, and yet most difficult to describe.

The tourist who is fond of practising the "gentle art," will find any quantity he is able and willing to fish for—the river abounding in fish of the most marvellous quantity and size. The angler will find plenty of excellent accommodation at Clayton or Alexandria Bay, with boats, etc. To enjoy a day or two amongst the Thousand Islands to the most advantage, is for the tourist to take up his quarters for a few days at either of these places, and sail amongst the islands with a row-boat. The tourist who is acquainted with the islands on "Lomond's Silver Loch," opposite Luss, in the Highlands of Scotland, will have some idea of what the Thousand Islands are — only that the latter extend fully 50 miles along the channel of the St. Lawrence, with some of the islands of much larger dimensions than those either on Loch Lomond or Loch Katrine. Names are given to some of the islands, whilst several have light-houses erected upon them.

With these remarks, we will now proceed, as if on board the American steamer, down the American channel, through them—there being one channel for the Canadian Company's boats, and another for the American Company's.

Leaving Kingston, the tourist in the Canadian Company's steamer will proceed on for six miles, and enter the regions of the Thousand Islands. For a description of the scenery of the route, we quote from a writer who thus describes it:

"These islands appear so thickly studded, that the appearance to the spectator, on approaching them, is as if the vessel steered her course towards the head of a landlocked bay which barred all further progress. Coming nearer, a small break in the line of shore opens up, and he enters between what he now discovers to be islands, and islands which are innumerable. Now, he sails in a wide channel be-

Leaving CAPE VINCENT, the steamer now proceeds towards the islands, and, after winding her course amongst them for about twenty miles, reaches the stopping-place called

CLAYTON, a small, well-built village, from which a considerable lumber trade is carried on, several rafts of which may probably be seen in French Creek, close at hand, ready for being "run" down the St. Lawrence to Montreal or Quebec. Several of the finest steamers which navigate the St. Lawrence were built here.

ALEXANDRIA BAY, 12 miles from Clayton, is soon reached—in approaching which, the tourist will admire the exquisite

25

THE THOUSAND ISLANDS ON THE ST. LAWRENCE.

FROM A PHOTOGRAPH TAKEN AT BROCKVILLE, CANADA WEST.

tween more distant shores; again, he enters into a strait so narrow that the large paddle-boxes of the steamer almost sweep the foliage, on either side, as she pursues her devious course. Now, the islands are miles in circumference; and again, he passes some which are very small, shaded by a single tiny tree occupying the handful of earth which represents the 'dry land.' On all, the trees grow to the water's edge, and dip their outer branches in the clear blue lake. Sometimes the *mirage* throws its air of enchantment on the whole, and the more distant islands seem floating in mid-heaven—only descending into the lake as a nearer approach dispels the illusion, and when the rushing steamer breaks the fair surface of the water in which all this loveliness is reflected, as in a mirror."

BROCKVILLE (Canada West) is the county town for the united counties of Leeds and Grenville. A steamer plies to Norristown, on the American side. All the American as well as Canadian steamers touch here. The tourist cannot fail to admire the fine location of Brockville, and its numerous tastefully laid out gardens, stretching down to the river's edge, as well as some neat built villas on the banks. Named after Gen. Brock, whose monument, at Queenstown Heights, commemorates his fall in battle there in 1812. Distant from Kingston 48 miles by rail, and Montreal 125 miles. The steamer, after leaving Brockville, proceeds for 12 miles, and reaches the town of

PRESCOTT, which is situated almost immediately opposite to Ogdensburg. At Prescott, both lines of steamers touch. From there, branches off the railroad to OTTAWA CITY—the future capital of Canada—a visit to which will well repay the tourist. 55 miles to Ottawa per railroad. Considerable amount of business is done with Ogdensburg, opposite, to and from which plies two ferry steamers. Population about 4,000. 113 miles from Montreal by rail.

One mile below Prescott is "Windmill Point," being the ruins of an old windmill, where, in 1837, the Canadian patriots, under a Polish exile named Von Shultz, established their headquarters, but were subsequently driven from it, with great loss.

scenery which now opens up to view on every turn which the steamer takes. From Alexandria Bay, some of the finest views of the islands, to our mind, are to be seen; whilst from the high points near the village, upwards of one hundred of the islands can be counted in one view. The situation of Alexandria Bay must always render it a favourite place with the tourist who delights in romantic situations or good sport. After steaming along for other 22 miles, the last of the Thousand Islands is seen, and the steamer touches on the Canadian side, at the thriving and prettily situated town of Brockvile (Canada West).

MORRISTOWN is situated exactly opposite Brockville, with which it is connected by steam ferry every half hour, 1 mile distance.

The American steamer, after leaving Brockville, proceeds on to

OGDENSBURG, now an important link in the chain of communication between the United States and Canada, with a railroad to Lake Champlain, (118 miles off) and which also connects at Rouse's Point with the other lines, to Boston and New York, as well as to Montreal. A considerable trade is done at Ogdensburg, whilst the situation of the town is one of the prettiest on the whole route. Settled by the French in 1748, attacked by the Mohawk Indians in 1749, and, on the defeat of Montcalm at Quebec, the settlement was abandoned by the French.

After Ogdensburg, comes Waddington, opposite to Ogden Island. Thirty miles further on is Louisville, from which stages run to Messina Springs, 7 miles distant.

The American steamer proceeds onwards to the first rapid in the route, known by the name of Gallop's Rapids, succeeded by others of lesser note. (See Descent of the Rapids.)

Four miles further on is Chimney Island, on which stands the ruin of an old French fortification. A short distance from there is

CHRYSELLER'S FARM, where a battle was fought between the Americans and the British, in 1813, at the time when the Americans, under Gen. Wilkinson, were descending the river to attack Montreal, but which attempt was afterwards abandoned.

ST. LAWRENCE CHANNEL OF THE

27

DESCENT OF THE RAPIDS.

AT LONG SAULT.

THESE Rapids, universally allowed to be the most extensive and the most exciting to be found on this continent, extend in continuous lines for a distance of nine miles—the stream being divided near its centre by an island. The channels on both sides are descended with safety, although steamers usually pass on the south side, which is a trifle narrower than the other. The current moves along this channel with astonishing velocity, drifting rafts at the rate of 12 or 14 miles an hour, the waters alone moving at least 20 miles an hour. It needs not the aid of wind or steam to descend these swift-sweeping waters, and hence when vessels enter the current they shut off steam, and trust to the guidance of the helm only as they are borne on their rapid voyage by the force of the stream alone. Nature presents but few sights more grand and beautiful than is presented from the deck of a steamer when descending these rapids. The unequal movement of the waves, as they plunge from one eddy to another, causes the boat to rise and fall with a motion not unlike that experienced on the ocean after a gale of wind has disturbed its bosom. The constant roar of the waters as they dash and leap along their furious course, filling the atmosphere with misty foam; the wild and tumultuous force with which wave struggles with wave to reach the depths below; the whirlings of the yawning eddies, that seem strong and angry enough to engulph any and every thing that ventures within their embrace, and the ever-changing features, form and course of the writhing, restless stream, all unite in presenting a scene of surpassing grandeur.

The navigation of these rapids, although generally conducted with entire safety, requires, nevertheless, great nerve, force and presence of mind on the part of the pilots—generally Indians—who essay to guide the staggering steamer on its course. It is imperative that the vessel should keep her head straight with the stream, for if she diverges in the least, so as to present her side to the current, she would be in-

ROUTE FROM PRESCOTT.

DOWN THE RAPIDS.

THE steamer, after leaving Prescott, proceeds, passing, on its way, between Chimney Island and Drummond's Island —now steering for Tick Island, thence northwest round the western end of Isle aux Galops, and by Fraser's Island to a point opposite Lock 27 of the canal, which extends from the beginning of the Gallop Rapids to Point Iroquois and rapids. Instead of passing through that canal, however, the steamer proceeds down the Gallop Rapids.

GALLOP RAPIDS.

IN sailing down these rapids, the steamer passes on its way Isle aux Galops, and several other small islands in the channel, onwards to Long Point—passing down the rapids between Tousson's Island and the south bank of the river; thence on again, and down the Iroquois Rapids, shortly after passing which we reach Ogden's Island, with rapids on each side of it. (At this point the *up* steamers ascend *via* the Rapide Platte Canal, from Lock 23 to 24.) After passing Ogden's Island, and several smaller ones, we pass Goose Neck Island and Crysler's Island, and proceed on between the two Cat Islands, the Upper Long Sault—now called Croyle's Island—and the rapids on the north-western end of it, at Farren's Point, where there is a short canal for the *up* steamer to pass through.

LONG SAULT RAPIDS.

SAILING down the rapid there, we pass at some distance Dickenson's Landing, close to Long Sault Island, and prepare to what is termed " shoot the Rapids of the Long Sault"—passing by the north channel, and downward through the rapids between Sheek's Island and Barnhart's Island. After steaming a short distance, with smooth sailing, we again reach rapids, being those between the town of Cornwall and Cornwall Island. (The *up* steamers enter in at Lock 15, at Cornwall, and passing along the canal with its eight locks, find an exit at **Lock 22**.) For a description of the passage

STEAMERS DESCENDING LOST CHANNEL, LONG SAULT RAPIDS, ST. LAWRENCE,

WITH STEAMER ASCENDING THE RIVER, VIA CANAL.

STEAMER DESCENDING ONE OF THE RAPIDS OF THE ST. LAWRENCE.

stantly capsized and lost. In order to prevent such catastrophies, boats traversing the rapids have their rudders constructed in such a manner that any amount of power can be brought to bear upon them at any moment. Not only is the wheel guided by strongly-wrought, but pliable chains, which are managed from a position near the bows, but a strong tiller is adjusted at the stern, which requires the aid of four powerful men, while two are working at the wheel, to keep the vessel's head in its proper direction.

The greatest danger attends the adventurous raftsmen, whose skill, courage and physical strength are perhaps not excelled by any similar body of men in the world. But, despite all these advantages, many a raft has been broken, and many a gallant raftsman's life has been lost upon this remorseless tide of waters.

down the Long Sault Rapids, see the opposite column on this page. For Illustration of the same, see engraving.

St. Regis is an old Indian village, one of the historical incidents connected with which, is a marauding excursion made by the St. Regis Indians, into Massachusetts, to recover a bell for their church, which, having been captured on its way to Canada from France, was purchased for the church of Deerfield, Massachusetts—but retaken from there by the said Indians, who claimed it as theirs, and who murdered, in the dead of night, 47, and captured 112, of the unsuspecting and innocent citizens of Deerfield. Having obtained the bell, they carried it, suspended from a pole, on their shoulders, for 150 miles, and it now hangs in the Catholic Church of St. Regis, built about 160 years ago.

Steamers in their passage *up* the St. Lawrence, when they come to the rapids, pass round them, by entering the stupendous canals which have been made for the purpose of enabling them to pass *up*, as well as *down*, the river—although it is in the passage *down* the river, such as we are now describing, in which all the beauty and enjoyment of the trip is to be seen and realized. Having passed through the most exciting part of the whole trip, we now arrive at the town of Cornwall, at the foot of the Long Sault Rapids—on the Canada side.

Cornwall is the boundary line between the United States and Canada, so that, after this point, all the points of interest remaining are now within the British possessions. Here the Cornwall Canal may be seen, 12 miles long, by which vessels pass up—as already mentioned.

LAKE ST. FRANCIS.

After leaving Cornwall, we proceed on, passing St. Regis Island, situated in mid-channel, until we enter Lake St. Francis, passing between the Squaw's Island and Butternut Islands, with lighthouse to the north, in Lancaster Shoal. The steamer now steers close to the floating light, onwards to Cherry Island Light, and passing McGee's Point Light, on the main land, (north shore,) sails on towards the Rapids of Coteau du Lac.

COTEAU RAPIDS AND CEDARS RAPIDS.

At the Coteau du Lac Rapids, a cluster of sixteen islands interrupt the regular navigation, but through which the skilful pilot steers first down the rapid between the main land and Giron Island, thence down again between French Island, and Maple and Thorn Islands, and again between Prisoner's Island and Broad Island,

Coteau du Lac "is a small village, situated at the foot of Lake St. Francis. The name, as well as the style of the buildings, denotes its French origin. Just below the village are the Coteau Rapids."

Cedars Rapids are situated between the village of Cedars (north shore) and village of St. Timothé, (south shore,) with 8 or 10

31

and emerging into smooth water along-side of Grand Island, until, shortly after, the Cedars Rapids are reached.

CEDARS.—This village presents the same marks of French origin as Coteau du Lac. In the expedition of Gen. Amherst, a detachment of three hundred men, that were sent to attack Montreal, were lost in the rapids near this place. "The passage through these rapids is very exciting. There is a peculiar motion of the vessel, which, in descending, seems like settling down, as she glides from one ledge to another. In passing the rapids of the Split Rock, a person, unacquainted with the navigation of these rapids, will almost involuntarily hold his breath until this ledge of rocks, which is distinctly seen from the deck of the steamer, is passed. At one time the vessel seems to be running directly upon it, and you feel certain that she will strike; but a skilful hand is at the helm, and in an instant more it is passed in safety."

small islands in the channel where the rapids are.

On the south side of the river is Beauharnois.

BEAUHARNOIS "is a small village at the foot of the Cascades, on the south bank of the river. (Here UP vessels enter the Beauharnois Canal—with nine locks—and pass around the rapids of the Cascades, Cedars and Coteau, into Lake St. Francis, a distance of 14 miles.) On the north bank, a branch of the Ottawa enters into the St. Lawrence."

After passing down the rapids at Cedars, the steamer again enters the smooth waters of the St. Lawrence, only, however, to be soon once more broken in upon by the Cascade Rapids.

THE CASCADE RAPIDS AND LAKE ST. LOUIS.

THE CASCADE RAPIDS are situated between Cascade's Point and Buisson Pointe, in which are situated Mary's Reef, Dog's Reef, Split Rock, Round Island and Isle aux Cascades. On the north side of these rapids, the majestic river Ottawa comes sweeping along, and round both sides of Isle Perrot, and here joins issue with the St. Lawrence, in Lake St. Louis. A smooth and pleasant sail of 24 miles along Lake St. Louis will be enjoyed, until the last rapids of all are reached, viz., Lachine.

The steamboat track proceeds through Lake St. Louis, passing three floating light-ships and the town of Lachine, on north bank, and Caughnawaga, on south bank of river.

LA CHINE.—This village is nine miles from Montreal, with which it is connected by railroad. "The La Chine Rapids begin just below the town. The current is here so swift and wild, that to avoid it a canal has been cut around these rapids. This canal is a stupendous work, and reflects much credit upon the energy and enterprise of the people of Montreal.

At La Chine is the residence of Sir George Simpson, Governor of the Hudson's Bay Company, and of the officers of this, the chief post of that corporation. It is from this point that the orders from head-quarters in London are sent to all the many posts throughout the vast territory of the company; and near the end of April

CAUGHNAWAGA.—"This is an Indian village, lying on the south bank of the river, near the entrance of the La Chine Rapids. It derived its name from the Indians that had been converted by the Jesuits, who were called "Caughnawagas," or "praying Indians." This was probably a misnomer, for they were distinguished for their predatory incursions upon their neighbours in the New England provinces. The Indians at Caughnawaga subsist chiefly by navigating barges and rafts down to Montreal, and, in winter, by a trade in moccasins, snow-shoes, etc. They are mostly Roman Catholics, and possess an elegant church."

Many of the Caughnawaga Indians are

RAFTS OF LUMBER "RUNNING" THE RAPIDS, AT CEDARS, ON THE ST. LAWRENCE.

each year a body of trained *voyageurs* set out hence in large canoes, called *maitres canots*, with packages and goods for the various posts in the wilderness. Two centuries ago, the companions of the explorer Cartier, on arriving here, thought they had discovered a route to China, and expressed their joy in the exclamation of La Chine! Hence the present name, or so at least says tradition."

to be met with on the steamers, and in the streets in the cities of Montreal, Quebec, and even in New York, selling their fancy bead-work, etc.

La Prairie is some seven miles below Caughnawaga, or Village of the Rapids, after which the steamer sails on for a few miles, and reaches the City of Montreal.

LACHINE RAPIDS.

Previous to entering the Lachine Rapids, the tourist may observe the entrance to the aqueduct of the water-works which supplies Montreal with water—a gigantic undertaking, and affording the citizens of that city a never-failing, unlimited supply of good *aqua*.

There are 7 small islands in the channel of the Lachine Rapids. The steamer passes on between Isle du Diable, Isle au Heron, and Isle Boket, and after passing down the rapids, the steamer proceeds along, passing near to Nun's Island, belonging to the Grey Nunnery, Montreal, and one of the many islands which belong, and yield large resources to, the nunneries. A slight rapid, named

NORMAN RAPID, is sailed through, and, after passing that great monument of engineering skill, the Victoria Bridge, the steamer lands her passengers at the wharf of the city of Montreal.

34

MONTREAL TO QUEBEC.

THE tourist who is desirous of proceeding on his voyage at once, only staying until after he has visited the commercial capital of Canada, and enjoyed the magnificent view from the mountain behind the City of Montreal, or from off the top of the Notre Dame in Place d'Armes, will find the Quebec steamers—comfortably fitted up and well appointed—ready to start every evening about six o'clock. From the fact of the steamers sailing both from Montreal and Quebec in the evening, a short time during daylight is only left for the traveller to see much of the river and its banks between these two cities. This need hardly be regretted, however, so much, as the scenery, for the most part, is tame and uninteresting —the chief attractions being the neat and picturesquely-situated French-Canadian villages, which are situated on its banks, here and there, the tin-covered spires of their churches in the clear moonlight night—the sailing of the steamer swiftly down the stream, and the beautiful moonlight on a still summer's night—all contribute to render such a trip pleasant, and a change from what is almost nowhere else to be enjoyed in any other trip which can be taken in Canada.

Leaving Montreal, therefore, by the steamer, a good view of the city and St. Helen's Island—in the middle of the stream—is to be seen. The island is fortified, and commands the passage of the river.

The RAPIDS OF ST. MARY are just below St. Helen's Island, and, although not dangerous, are very troublesome to the river craft, which are much retarded in their movements by these obstinate rapids.

The first village passed is that of Longueil—three miles below Montreal, on south side of the river—the terminus of the Grand Trunk Railroad to Portland and Quebec.

LONGUE POINT AND POINT AUX TREMBLES, on the Island of Montreal, are successively passed on the left, and BOUCHERVILLE on the opposite shore.

The ISLAND OF ST. THERESA is 15 miles below the city, and near the mouth of Ottawa River.

VARENNES, on the south-east side of the river, is a beautiful village, which is often resorted to on account of the mineral springs to be found in its vicinity.

WILLIAM HENRY, or SOREL, 30 miles below Varennes, is a town of some 3000 inhabitants. It stands on the site of an old fort built in 1665, at the mouth of Richelieu River, and the first permanent settlement was made in 1685. The "fort" was taken, and occupied in May, 1776, by a party of Americans, in their retreat from Quebec, on the death of Gen. Montgomery.

Leaving *Richelieu River*, which is the outlet of Lake Champlain into the St. Lawrence, we pass a succession of small islands, and enter

LAKE ST. PETER'S.

THIS lake, which is formed by an expansion of the river, is about twenty-five miles long and nine miles broad, but is, for the most part, rather shallow. Recent improvements, however, have rendered the navigation such that the largest sailing vessels, and the Canadian and Liverpool steamers now pass up during the summer season to Montreal. Like all the other lakes, that of St. Peter's assumes a very different appearance in the summer season, during mild weather, from what it does during a gale of wind. Then it presents all the appearance, as well as the dangers of the sea, and rafts on their way down the river are frequently wrecked on its waters—the violence of the winds and waves being such as to render the rafts unmanageable, and part them asunder, to the loss sometimes of life as well as the timber.

On the south bank of the river is the small village of Port St. Francis, 82 miles from Montreal.

Proceeding on for other eight miles, the steamer stops at one of the oldest settled towns in Canada, viz.:

THREE RIVERS, 90 miles from Montreal, being half way between Quebec and Montreal. Situated at the confluence of the St. Lawrence and River St. Maurice. Population about 5000. The most prominent buildings are the Roman Catholic and Protestant churches, a convent, jail, and court-house. Founded in 1618. After leaving Three Rivers the steamer proceeds onwards, and shortly passes the mouth of the St. Maurice River, which enters the St. Lawrence from Canada. The beautiful stream runs a course of some 400 miles in a south-east direction, frequently expanding and forming lakes of various sizes. Its banks are generally very high, varying from 200 to 1,000 feet, and covered with thick groups of variegated trees. It has a number of falls and cascades, and is adorned with several small islands. Its principal tributaries are the Ribbon and Vermillion, running from the west, and the Windigo and Croche Rivers, from the east. The next town reached is

BATISCAN, on the same side of the river, 117 miles from Montreal, and the last stopping-place before arriving at Quebec. Batiscan is reached at an early hour in the morning.

RICHELIEU RAPIDS.—The channel of the river where these rapids occur is very narrow and intricate, huge irregular rocks being visible in many places during low water. Beacon lights are placed at the most dangerous points, to aid the mariner in navigating these difficult passages, which extend a distance of 8 or 9 miles.

Pursuing our course, we pass the small settlements of St. Marie, St. Anne, Point Aux Trembles, and Port Neuf, on the north, and Gentilly, St. Pierre, Dechellons, Lothinière, and St. Croix, on the south side of the river. Nearly opposite St. Croix is Cape Sante.

CAPE SANTE is about 30 miles above Quebec, on the north side of the river; a small settlement called St. Trois being on the opposite shore. The banks of the river rise here almost perpendicularly to a height of 80 feet above the water, and extend back for many miles with an almost level surface.

CAPE ROUGE, 8 miles above Quebec, is next passed on the left, when the citadel of Quebec comes into view, presenting a sight at once grand and deeply interesting, from its historical associations.

CHAUDIERE RIVER, on the right, has a number of beautiful falls a short distance from its entrance into the St. Lawrence.

WOLF'S COVE, 2 miles above Quebec, is historically famous as the place where the immortal *Wolfe* landed with his gallant army in 1759, and ascended to the Plains of Abraham, where the heroic chief fell mortally wounded, just at the successful termination of one of the most daring enterprises ever chronicled in the annals of warfare.

On the opposite side of the river is Point Levi, a small town of about 1500 inhabitants. Here is the Quebec station of the Grand Trunk Railroad.

On approaching Quebec the character of the country again resumes a more picturesque appearance—the high banks and finely-wooded country showing to great advantage. Within a few miles of the City of Quebec some private residences may be seen embosomed amid the foliage, in romantic situations, on the heights above, on the north side of the river, and on nearing the city the port of New Liverpool may be seen on the right-hand, or south side of the river, with some large ships lying at anchor there, as well as all the way between there and Quebec; where, during the season of open navigation, immense numbers of large vessels may be seen waiting to discharge their cargoes, and load the timber of Canada for transportation to all parts of the world, but more particularly to Greenock, on the River Clyde, (Scotland,) and Liverpool, on the Mersey, (England).

Previous to arriving, the spot may be seen on the face of the embankment where the gallant Montgomery was killed whilst attempting to storm the citadel at that point.

The steamer, after rounding the high cliffs and Cape Diamond, takes a sweep round in the river, and lands its passengers, about seven o'clock in the morning, at the base of the Citadel of Quebec—the "Gibraltar of America."

CITY OF QUEBEC—CANADA EAST.

ASSOCIATED as Quebec is with so many scenes of military glory, of success as well as defeat, it must at all times possess a peculiar interest to almost every one. On its fields, and

around its battlements, some of the bravest of the sons of Great Britain and Ireland, America and France, have fallen, and around its citadel, some of the most daring exploits have taken place. Standing on a bold and precipitous promontory, Quebec has not inappropriately been called the "Gibraltar of America," with which the names of the brave Wolfe, Montcalm, and Montgomery must ever remain connected.

The citadel stands on what is called Cape Diamond, 350 feet above the level of the sea, and includes about 40 acres of ground. The view from off the citadel is of the most picturesque and grand character. There will be seen the majestic St. Lawrence, winding its course for about 40 miles, whilst the background of the panoramic scene is filled up by extensive plains, running backwards to lofty mountains in the distance, with Point Levi opposite, and the Island of Orleans in the distance, whilst the junction of the River St. Charles, and the Great River, form that magnificent sheet of water, where numerous vessels are to be seen riding at anchor during the summer season.

A walk around the ramparts of the citadel will well repay the stranger, by a magnificent change of scene at every turn he takes. The city itself bears all the resemblance of a strongly fortified and ancient city, and, in that respect, so very different from the newly sprung-up cities, westward. The streets are generally narrow, and, in some parts, very steep, in walking from Lower Town to Upper Town, more particularly. Lower Town is where all the shipping business of the port is carried on, chiefly lumber—in export—and every description of goods—in import. At Quebec, the greater portion of the immense lumber-district of the Ottawa finds a market; vessels coming to Quebec, in ballast and cargo, return with the logs, staves, and deals of the up-country. The population of Quebec is largely infused with French Canadians, and in passing along its streets, nothing, almost, but the French language is heard.

The most interesting places and objects of interest in and around Quebec will be found as follows:—

The Plains of Abraham, a short way out of the city, westward, where the celebrated battle was fought between the troops of Britain and France, led by their heroes Wolfe and Montcalm. A monument is erected on the spot where Wolfe fell, with the inscription, "Here Wolfe died victorious."

The Citadel, situated on the highest point of Cape Diamond, and commanding the most extensive view to be had.

The Esplanade, between the ramparts and D'Autueil street, used for drilling the troops.

DURHAM TERRACE AND THE CITADEL, QUEBEC.

The Public, or Palace Garden, in Upper Town, fronts Des Curriers street. One of the most interesting objects of historical interest is the granite monument erected to the joint memory of the two opposing heroes, Wolfe and Montcalm, who both fell in battle. It is placed in what is called the Palace Garden, finely shaded with trees. It was erected in 1827; the Earl of Dalhousie, then Governor-general of Canada, laying the foundation-stone amid great masonic honors. The chaste design of the monument, which is 65 feet high, is

WOLFE AND MONTCALM'S MONUMENT.

QUEBEC.

from the pencil of Captain Young, 79th Highlanders, and the concise but eloquent inscription is by Dr. J. C. Fisher, at one time connected with the Quebec press, for which inscription he was awarded a gold medal. It reads as follows:

WOLFE—MONTCALM.

MORTEM VIRTUS COMMUNEM;

FAMAM HISTORIA ;

MONUMENTUM POSTERITAS.

DEDIT.

A. D. 1827.

Which, being rendered into English, means: "Military virtue gave them a common death history a common fame; posterity a common monument."

39

QUEBEC.

Durham Terrace, from which one of the finest and most extensive views is to be had. A great resort of the citizens during the cool evenings of summer. At one time the site of the Castle of St. Louis.

The Marine Hospital, situated on the peninsula near Cartier's Bay; the spot where Jacques Cartier, the discoverer of the St. Lawrence, spent the winter of 1535 and '36.

The Ruins of the Intendant Palace, near Craig street, may interest the antiquary in such matters. *Montcalm's Head-quarters*, on the heights of Beauport, a short way east of Beauport's Mills. *Montmorenci House*, situated close to the bank of the river, near the Falls of Montmorenci, once the residence of the late Duke of Kent, father of her present Majesty Queen Victoria. *The Quebec Exchange*, an excellent reading-room, well supplied with Canadian, American and British newspapers. Free to strangers.

The University of Quebec, Hope street, Upper Town, a massive gray stone building.

Court House and City Hall, St. Louis street.

Jail, corner of Ann street. Cost £60,000 ($300,000).

The Jesuit Barracks, Lunatic Asylum, Music Hall, and the Protestant and Catholic churches form the remainder of the principal buildings in the city.

"A morning's ramble to the Plains of Abraham will not fail to recall historical recollections and to gratify a taste for beautiful scenery. On leaving the St. Louis Gate, let the traveller ascend the counterscarp on the left, that leads to the *glacis* of the citadel; and hence pursuing a direction to the right, let him approach one of the Martello Towers, whence he may enjoy a beautiful view of the St. Lawrence. A little beyond let him ascend the right bank, and he reaches the celebrated Plains of Abraham, near the spot where General Wolfe fell. On the highest ground, surrounded by wooden fences, can clearly be traced out the redoubt where he received the fatal wound. He was carried a few yards in the rear, and placed against a rock till he expired. It has since been removed. Within an enclosure lower down, and near to the road, is the stone well from which they brought him water. The English right nearly faced this redoubt, and on this position the French left rested. The French army arrived on the Plains from the right of this position, as it came from Beauport, and not from Quebec; and, on being defeated, retired down the heights by which it had ascended, and not into Quebec. In front of the Plains from this position stands the house of Marchmont. It is erected on the sight of a French redoubt that once defended the ascent from Wolfe's Cove. Here landed the British army under Wolfe's command, and, on mounting the banks, carried this detached work. The troops in the garrison are usually reviewed on the Plains. The tourist may farther enjoy a beautiful ride. Let him leave by St. Louis Gate and pass the Plains, and he will arrive at Marchmont, the property of John Gilmour, Esq. The former proprietor, Sir John Harvey, went to considerable expense in laying out the grounds in a pleasing and tasteful manner. His successor, Sir Thomas Noel Hill, also resided here, and duly appreciated its beauties. The view in front of the house is grand. Here the river widens, and assumes the appearance of a lake, whose surface is enlivened by numerous merchant-ships at anchor, and immense rafts of timber floating down. On leaving Marchmont he will pass some beautiful villas, whose park-like grounds remind one of England, and from some points in which are commanded views worthy of a painter's study. Among these villas may be mentioned Wolfesfield, Spencer Wood, and Woodfield. The last was originally built by the Catholic Bishop of Samos, and, from the several additions made by subsequent proprietors, had a somewhat irregular, though picturesque appearance. It was burnt down, and rebuilt in a fine regular style. It is now the residence of James Gibb, Esq.

"In this neighbourhood is situated Mount Hermon Cemetery. It is about three miles from Quebec, on the south side of the St. Lewis road, and slopes irregularly but beautifully down the cliff which overhangs the St. Lawrence. It is thirty-two acres in extent, and the grounds were tastefully laid out by the late Major Douglass, U. S. Engineers, whose taste and skill had been previously shown in the arrangement of Greenwood Cemetery, near New York."

Leaving this beautiful locality, the walk continues to the woods, on the edge of the banks rising from the shore.

The tourist, instead of returning by a road conducting through a wood into St. Louis Road for Quebec, would do better by continuing his ride to the Church of St. Foy, from which is seen below the St. Charles, gliding smoothly through a lovely valley, whose sides rise gradually to the mountains, and are literally covered with habitations. The villages of Lorette and Charlesbourg are conspicuous objects. Before entering the suburb of St. John, on the banks of the St. Charles stands the General Hospital, designed, as the name implies, for the disabled and sick of every description.

A day's excursion to Indian Lorette and Lake St. Charles would gratify, we doubt not, many a tourist. It will be necessary to leave by 6 o'clock, A. M., and to take provisions for the trip. After leaving the Palace Gate, the site of the former intendant's palace is passed. Mr. Bigot was the last intendant who resided in it.

The most pleasant road to Lorette is along the banks of the St. Charles. On arriving at the village, the best view is on the opposite bank. The fall is in the foreground, and the church and village behind. The villagers claim to be descended from those Hurons, to whom the French monarch, in 1651, gave the seigniory of Sillery. In the wars between the French and English, the Hurons contributed much to the success of the former, as they were one of the most warlike tribes among the aborigines of this continent. At present, they are a harmless, quiet set of people, drawing only part of their subsistence from fishing and hunting. A missionary is maintained by government for their religious instruction, and the schoolmaster belongs to the tribe. Here may be purchased bows and arrows, and moccasins very neatly ornamented by the squaws.

On arriving at Lake St. Charles, by embarking in a double canoe, the tourist will have his taste for picturesque mountain scenery gratified in a high degree. The lake is four miles long, and one broad, and is divided into two parts by projecting ledges. The lake abounds in trout, so that the angling tourist may find this spot doubly inviting. On the route back to the city, the village of Charlesbourg is passed. It is one of the oldest and most interesting settlements in Canada. It has two churches, one of which is the centre of the surrounding farms, whence they all radiate. The reason for this singular disposal of the allotments, arose from the absolute necessity of creating a neighbourhood. For this purpose, each farm was permitted to occupy only a space of three acres in front by thirty in depth. The population was in these days scanty, and labourers were difficult to be procured. By this arrangement, a road was more equally kept up in front of each farm, and it was the duty of every proprietor to preserve such road. Another advantage was the proximity of the church, whence the bell sounded the tocsin of alarm, whenever hostile attempts were made by the Indians, and where the inhabitants rallied in defence of their possessions.

Within the citadel are the various magazines, store-houses, and other buildings required for the accommodation of a numerous garrison; and immediately overhanging the precipice to the south, in a most picturesque situation, looking perpendicularly downwards, on the river, stands a beautiful row of buildings, containing the mess rooms and barracks for the officers, their stables, and spacious kitchens. The fortifications, which are continued round the whole of the Upper Town, consist of bastions connected by lofty curtains of solid masonry, and ramparts from 25 to 35 feet in height, and about the same in thickness, bristling with heavy cannon, round towers, loophole walls, and massive gates recurring at certain distances. On the summit of the ramparts, from Cape Diamond to the Artillery Barracks, is a broad covered way, or walk, used as a place of recreation by the inhabitants, and commanding a most agreeable view of the country towards the west. This passes over the top of St. John's and St. Louis Gate, where there is stationed a sergeant's guard. Above St. John's Gate, there is at sunset one of the most beautiful views imaginable. The St. Charles gambolling, as it were, in the rays of the departing luminary, the light still lingering on the spires of Lorette and Charlesbourg, until it fades away beyond the lofty mountains of *Bonhomme* and *Tsounonthuan*, present an evening scene of gorgeous and surpassing splendour. The city, being defended on its land side by its ramparts, is protected on the other sides by a lofty wall and parapet, based on the cliff, and commencing near the St. Charles at the Artillery Barracks. These form a very extensive range of buildings, the part within the Artillery Gate being occupied as barracks by the officers and men of that distinguished corps, with a guard and mess room. The part without the gate is used as magazines, store-houses, and offices for the ordnance department.

The circuit of the fortifications, enclosing the Upper Town, is two miles and three-quarters; the total circumference outside the ditches and space reserved by government, on which no house can be built on the west side, is about 3 miles.

Founded upon a rock, and in its highest parts overlooking a great extent of country—between 300 and 400 miles from the ocean—in the midst of a great continent, and yet displaying fleets of foreign merchantmen in its fine capacious bay, and showing all the bustle of a crowded sea-port—its streets narrow, populous, and winding up and down almost mountainous declivities—situated in the latitude of the finest parts of Europe—exhibiting in its environs the beauty of an European capital—and yet, in winter, smarting with the cold of Siberia—governed by a people of different language and habits from the mass of the population—opposed in religion, and yet leaving that population without taxes, and in the full enjoyment of every privilege, civil and religious. Such are the prominent features which strike a stranger in the City of Quebec!"

The stranger can have no difficulty in finding the various places and objects of interest in, and around the city, and by taking a *caleche*, and making a bargain beforehand, will be able to see a great deal in little time, and at no great cost.

For particulars of the Falls of Montmorenci, and River Saguenay, see following pages.

42

CITY OF MONTREAL, C. E.

THE stranger, on approaching Montreal, either from Quebec by the steamer, or crossing over from the opposite side of the river, in coming from the States, will at once be impressed favorably with the situation of the city, the business-like appearance it presents, and the picturesque scenery by which it is surrounded.

Montreal is the most populous city in Canada, and in every respect must take the first rank in the province. It is situated on the *Island* of Montreal—which is represented as the garden of Canada, being the richest soil in the province—at the head of ocean steamship navigation, and beyond which no large sailing vessels go, although smaller vessels pass on, via the canals and St. Lawrence, to the west.

The city is built of a gray limestone, having very much the appearance of Aberdeen granite, with buildings of great solidity and excellence in design. The chief business street is that of Notre Dame, whilst Great St. James street exceeds it in handsome buildings, besides being much broader. (See engraving.)

The wholesale stores are situated on the wharves alongside the river, and streets running parallel therewith.

Montreal is the port at which arrives the great bulk of the importations from Great Britain and other places abroad, being there either re-sold or transhipped to all parts of Canada East and West; consequently a large wholesale trade is carried on at Montreal in all descriptions of goods.

In the conglomerate mass of buildings there concentrated, are stores, churches, groceries, and nunneries, all intermixed with each other, whilst in the streets may be seen the manufacturer's cart driving alongside of the Catholic priest in his " brggy," the merchant's clerk hurrying on past a sister of charity or nun at large, and Frenchmen, Scotchmen, Germans, and Americans, all elbowing each other in the busy streets of the city *par excellence*. No better sample of this heterogeneous gathering is to be seen than by paying a visit to the Rue Notre Dame, or Bonsecours Market, where, on a Saturday night, a mixture of English, French, German, and broad Scotch, will fall upon the ear with peculiar effect.

Although one of the finest views of the city is obtained from off the mountain, undoubtedly the most extensive one is to be had from the top of the Catholic cathedral, in the Place d'Armes. By paying 1s. stg. you will be conducted to the top, and, if a fine day, the view is such as will well repay the ascent.

There are some very handsome churches in Montreal. At Beaver Hall, St. Andrew's Church (Presbyterian), and the Unitarian Church there, form two of the most prominent in the city, situated as they are on a considerable elevation, on rising ground. The public buildings of Montreal are substantial and elegant, and consist of—

PUBLIC BUILDINGS.

THE NEW COURT HOUSE, on Notre Dame street, and directly opposite to Nelson's Monument, is of elegant cut stone, in the Grecian Ionic style. The ground plan is 300 feet by 125 feet; height, 76 feet.

THE NEW POST-OFFICE, on Great St. James street, is a beautiful cut stone building.

THE MERCHANTS' EXCHANGE READING ROOM, situated on St. Sacrament street.

THE MECHANICS' INSTITUTE, a very fine building, situated on Great St. James street, of cut stone, 3 stories high, built in the Italian style. The Lecture Room is 60 by 80 feet, height 18 feet, neatly and tastefully finished.

THE MERCANTILE LIBRARY ASSOCIATION, Odd Fellows' Hall, opposite the above.

THE BANK OF MONTREAL, Place d'Armes, St. James street, opposite the Cathedral, an elegant cut stone building of the Corinthian order. (See engraving.)

THE CITY BANK, next to the above, in the Grecian style, of cut stone and worthy of note.

THE BANK OF BRITISH NORTH AMERICA, Great St. James street, next the Post-office, is a handsome building of cut stone, and built in the composite style of architecture.

EAST END.

CENTRE.

WEST END.

CENTRE.

CITY OF MONTREAL.—From the Mountain.

THE BONSECOURS MARKET, on St. Paul and Water streets, is a magnificent edifice. (See engraving.)

THE ST. ANN'S MARKET, opposite the Grey Nunnery.

THE GREY NUNNERY is situated on Foundling street, designed for the care of foundlings and infirm.

THE HOTEL DIEU NUNNERY, on St. Joseph and St. Paul streets, designed for sick and diseased persons.

THE CONVENT OF THE SISTERS OF THE SACRED HEART is situated at St. Vincent de Paul, 9 miles from Montreal.

ACADEMY OF THE SISTERS OF THE CONGREGATION DE NOTRE DAME, now Maria Villa, about 3 miles from Montreal, was formerly the residence of the Governor-General.

THE McGILL COLLEGE.—This is an institution of very high repute, founded by the Hon. James McGill, who bequeathed a valuable estate and £10,000 for its endowment. The buildings for the Faculty of Arts are delightfully situated at the base of the mountain, and command an extensive view.

THE MUSEUM OF THE NATURAL HISTORY OF MONTREAL, is situated in Little St. James street, and is free to strangers.

THE NEW CITY WATER WORKS.—These works tap the St. Lawrence at the Lachine Rapids, some 6 miles above the city, and will cost, when fully completed, nearly $1,000,000. The 2 receiving reservoirs, for supplying the city are about 200 feet above the level of the river, and hold 20,000,000 gallons.

THE JAIL.—This is a substantial stone building, surrounded by a high wall, and is worthy of a visit. It has recently been erected, at an expense of $120,000.

THE GENERAL HOSPITAL, on Dorchester street, is a fine cut stone building, and is one of the many prominent institutions of the city.

THE ST. PATRICK'S HOSPITAL, at the west end of the same street, is an elegant structure, and occupies a commanding position.

THE PROTESTANT ORPHAN ASYLUM, situated in Catherine street, is a well-conducted charity, sustained by the benevolence of private individuals.

THE LADIES' BENEVOLENT INSTITUTION, for the relief of widows and half orphans, is a large three-story building in Berthelot street. It is managed solely by a committee of ladies.

NELSON'S MONUMENT, Jacques Cartier square, Notre Dame street.

THE LACHINE CANAL is among the public works worthy of note.

PLACE D'ARMES is a handsome square, between Notre Dame and Great St. James streets, opposite the French Cathedral.

As a place of beauty and pleasure, the ride from the city to MOUNT ROYAL will attract the traveller at all times. The distance around it is 9 miles, commanding one of the finest views of beautiful landscape to be found in North America; and in returning, entering the city, a view of the St. Lawrence and of Montreal, both comprehensive and extended, that well repays the time and expense.

MOUNT ROYAL CEMETERY, about 2 miles from the city, on the mountain, is one of the places of interest about the city which many parties visit.

THE CHAMP DE MARS is a public parade ground, situated in Gabriel street, off Notre Dame. In the evenings, sometimes, the military bands play there, to a large concourse of the inhabitants.

THE VICTORIA BRIDGE.

This gigantic undertaking forms one of the most interesting and wonderful features connected with the city, at Point St. Charles.

It is being built for the purpose of enabling the Grand Trunk Railway to form a continuous railroad communication with the railroads of the United States, instead of passengers being obliged to cross the river in steamers, as at present.

The width of the river where the bridge is being built is very nearly 2 miles.

THE VICTORIA TUBULAR BRIDGE, ACROSS THE ST. LAWRENCE, MONTREAL.

TOTAL LENGTH WILL BE 10,284 FEET, OR ABOUT 50 YARDS LESS THAN 2 MILES, NOW BUILDING.

SOUTH SIDE OF GREAT ST. JAMES' STREET.

The first building on left side of the street is the General Post-office—54 by 100 feet—built in the Italian style. The third building in view is the Bank of British North America—which, with the Post-office, forms two of the finest buildings in the street. Still further on, is the Mechanics' Library, a substantial, plain, square block, with an excellent reading-room, library, and hall for lectures, etc.

PLACE D'ARMES, ST. JAMES' STREET.

The building with the beautiful fluted columns of the Corinthian order, represented above, is the Bank of Montreal—one of the finest buildings in the city. The next building to it is the City Bank of Montreal, an establishment with a much plainer exterior, in the Grecian style. Still further on, are some very elegant stores, with the Wesleyan Chapel in the distance, nearer the far end of the street.

BONSECOURS MARKET.

This is the largest, and one of the finest buildings in the city. Erected at a cost of $287,300. Used as a public market for the most part, where are sold an extraordinary quantity of provisions, vegetables, fruit, fish, besides clothing, "Yankee Notions," and an *omnium gatherum* of almost every thing required for domestic purposes. One portion of the building is used as a police station, as well as offices connected with the municipal government. It is situated close to the river side. Built in the Grecian-Doric style of architecture.

HAYMARKET AND BEAVER HALL.

The above view represents the Haymarket, with Beaver Hall in the back rising ground, which, in its number of handsome churches, presents one of the finest views in the city—more particularly in summer—with the mountain rising up behind, and filling up the back-ground of the picture with the luxuriant foliage of its shrubbery. The church with the highest spire in the above engraving, is that of St. Andrew's (Church of Scotland). The one seen in the corner to the right, is a very handsome church, now completing for the Unitarian congregation.

The current of the river is very rapid—with a depth of from 4 to 10 feet, excepting in the main channel, where it is from 30 to 35 feet deep.

In the winter, the ice is formed into a great thickness, and frequently immense piles accumulate—as high as 30 to 40 feet. Thus piled up in huge boulders, the water rushes through them at a fearful rate, driving the blocks of ice along, and crushing all before them.

The bridge will consist of 24 strong piers, standing 242 feet apart, excepting the centre span, which is 339 feet wide. They are all perpendicular on three sides, and slope down to the water-edge against the current, so as to withstand the force and action of the floating masses of ice, on its breaking up. Each pier is estimated to withstand the force of 70,000 tons of ice at one time.

Resting on these piers, and running from abutment to abutment, is the bridge, which consists of a hollow iron tube, 22 feet high, and 16 feet wide.

The centre span is to be 50 feet above the average level of the water, thence sinking towards each end 1 foot in 130, thus making the height of the abutments about 37 feet.

The estimated cost is about £1,250,000 stg. The weight of the iron in the tubes will be 8,000 tons, and the contents of the masonry will be about 3,000,000 cubic feet. The whole will be completed in the autumn of 1859 or spring of 1860. As is well known, the engineer of this greatest bridge in the world is Mr. Robert Stephenson of Newcastle-upon-Tyne.

48

MONTREAL TO OTTAWA, C. W.

This beautiful route may be traversed either by rail from Montreal to Prescott Junction, and thence by rail to Ottawa, as described elsewhere; or it may be taken by way of rail to Lachine, steamer from Lachine to Carrillon, rail from Carrillon to Grenville, and Grenville to Ottawa by steamer again. By this route it will be seen that there are several changes to be made, which cannot be avoided, on account of the rapids on the river, which cannot be "run" by the steamer.

This route is one so little known, that, notwithstanding the disadvantages which changing so often presents, we have thought it advisable to give a brief account of the trip to Ottawa, as made by us last June, addressing ourselves as if the reader were going. Proceeding in cab or omnibus to Griffintown — 1¼ miles from post-office, Montreal—you arrive and book at the Lachine Railroad Depot; fare through to Ottawa, first class, $3; second class, $2. Strange to say, no baggage is "checked through," on this route as via Grand Trunk railroad, or the other lines in the United States.

Started on the cars, therefore, with a string of tickets to and from the different points on your way, you soon reach Lachine, nine miles off. At Lachine you change cars, and step on board the steamer "Lady Simpson" in waiting, and once under weigh, you get a fine view of the mighty St. Lawrence, with Lake St. Louis close at hand.

Not long after the steamer starts, breakfast will be announced, which may be partaken of, if you had not got it before you started from Montreal. An excellent breakfast for 1s. 10½d. currency, (1s. 6d. stg.,) or 37½ cents. If a fine morning, you will be delighted with the sail, as the steamer skims along the shore of the Island of Montreal, till she reaches St. Anne's, at the extreme corner of that island. At St. Anne's, the steamer leaves the St. Lawrence, and passes through the locks there, and is then on the bosom of the Ottawa. You will scarcely be able to imagine it to be a river; in reality, it forms the Lake of the Two Mountains, being one of the numerous lakes which the Ottawa may be said to be a succession of.

At St. Anne's you will get an excellent view of the substantial stone bridge of the Grand Trunk Railway, which here crosses the Ottawa, and which forms a striking contrast to the mistaken policy of the railway companies in the United States in building so many "rickety" wooden bridges—with their warnings up of fines of so much if you trot a horse over them—and which in going over so many accidents have occurred. Here, possibly, you may observe, against one of the piers of this bridge, a portion of a large raft, which, in "running" the rapids last season, became unmanageable and dashed up against the bridge—scattering the raft in all directions—to the great loss of the proprietor of it. Some of the logs may be seen yet, resting up against the pier of the bridge, as if trying to clear all before them, and the gigantic pier standing up, in its mighty strength, as if bidding them float quietly past.

St. Anne's is the spot where the poet Moore located the scene of his celebrated Canadian Boat Song.

CANADIAN BOAT SONG.
BY THOMAS MOORE.

Faintly as tolls the evening chime,
Our voices keep tune and our oars keep time;
Soon as the woods on shore look dim,
We'll sing at St. Anne's our parting hymn.
    Row, brothers, row, the stream runs fast,
    The Rapids are near, and the daylight's past.

Why should we yet our sail unfurl?
There is not a breath the blue wave to curl;
But when the wind blows off the shore,
Oh! sweetly we'll rest our weary oar.
    Blow, breezes, blow, the stream runs fast,
    The Rapids are near, and the daylight's past.

Ottawa's tide ! this trembling moon
Shall see us float over thy surges soon.
Saint of this green isle ! hear our prayers,
Oh ! grant us cool heavens and favoring airs.
Blow, breezes, blow, the stream runs fast,
The Rapids are near, and the daylight's past.

Started from St. Anne's you shortly reach a beautiful expansion of the Ottawa—which forms here what is called THE LAKE OF THE TWO MOUNTAINS—named from the two mountains which are seen to the north, rising four hundred to five hundred feet high.

After sailing a short time, and with your face to the bow of the steamer, you will observe, to the right, where this great river—coming slowly and silently along—is divided by the Island of Montreal; the one fork of the river which you observe to the north-east, winding its way past the island, after which it makes its acquaintance with the St. Lawrence, to the north-east of Montreal. The other fork, or division on which you have just started from, at St. Anne's, meets the St. Lawrence there ; although, strange to say, the waters of these two immense rivers—as if not relishing the mixture of each other, and thus forming one—continue their separate and undivided distinctness for miles, till they meet with such rough treatment, from either torrents, wind, or waves, that they join issue, and form at last, one immense river in the St. Lawrence, in which the beautiful but majestic Ottawa is swallowed up.

In the last report on the Geological Survey of Canada, the following remarks on the component parts, and other peculiarities, of the Ottawa and St. Lawrence occur :—

"The water of the Ottawa, containing but little more than one-third as much solid matter as the St. Lawrence, is impregnated with a much larger portion of organic matter, derived from the decomposition of vegetable remains, and a large amount of alkalies uncombined with chlorine or sulphuric acid. Of the alkalies determined as chlorids, the chlorid of potassium in the Ottawa water forms thirty-two per cent., and in that of the St. Lawrence, only sixteen per cent.; while in the former, the silicia equals thirty-four per cent., and in the latter, twenty-three per cent., of the mineral matters. The Ottawa drains a region of crystalline rocks, and receives from these by far the greater part of its waters; hence the salts of potash, liberated by the decomposition of these rocks, are in large proportion. The extensive vegetable decomposition, evidenced by the organic matters dissolved in the water, will also have contributed a portion of potash. It will be recollected that the proportion of potash salts in the chlorids of sea-water and saline waters, generally, does not equal more than two or three per cent. As to the St. Lawrence, although the basin of Lake Superior, in which the river takes its origin, is surrounded by ancient sandstones, and by crystalline rocks, it afterwards flows through lakes whose basins are composed of palæozoic strata, which abound in limestones rich in gypsum and salt, and these rocks have given the waters of this river that predominance of soda, chlorine, and sulphuric acid which distinguishes it from the Ottawa. It is an interesting geographical feature of these two rivers, that they each pass through a series of great lakes, in which the waters are enabled to deposit their suspended impurities, and thus are rendered remarkably clear and transparent."

The two rivers thus not mixing at once, is owing, we presume, to the specific gravity of the one being much heavier than that of the other. The two are distinctly seen flowing down together, by the difference in their color.

The lake you are now upon—if a fine morning, and in summer—will be as calm as a mill-pond, and, with its wooded islands, and nicely-wooded country round about, forms a scene of the finest character. Each turn the steamer takes, it opens up with it new beauties. Sometimes, however, the lake, now so placid and beautiful to look upon, is raised like a raging sea, rendering its navigation not so easy, as many a poor raftsman has found to his cost, whilst navigating his treasure of lumber to Quebec or Lachine. You may, possibly, see some of these rafts of lumber as you pass along. Nowhere in the whole of America, we believe, will you see such magnificent and valuable rafts of lumber as on the Ottawa. The rafts on the Delaware, Ohio, and Mississippi, which we have seen, are nothing to compare to them—either in size or in the value of the wood of which they are composed.

Passing onwards on the lake, you will observe THE INDIAN VILLAGE, at the base of the Two Mountains. There reside the remnants of two tribes, the Iroquois and Algonquins.

On the sandy soil behind the village, the Indians have their games, foot races, etc., etc.

After passing there, the steamer will probably stop at VAUDREUL, at the head of the Lake of the Two Mountains. Proceeding on from there, the steamer will steer for Point Anglais, (English Point,) and from there cross over to the settlement of REGAUD, and a hill of the same name, on the river Le Graisse.

After enjoying the beauties of the scene on every side, you will shortly find yourself at Carrillon. Opposite Carrillon is situated Point Fortune, the station which leads per stage to the Caledonia Springs, unless passengers wish to go there from L'Original, which you will reach, by-and-by, by taking the cars at Carrillon, the point you have now reached.

At Carrillon you will leave the steamer, walk up to the train which is in readiness to convey you from there to Grenville. On alighting from the steamer, look after your baggage—see it placed on the cart which is to convey it from there to the train—and then see it placed on the train.

You will have a few minutes to wait at Carrillon, during which time you can be surveying the beauties of the scene around you—and get a peep of the rapids which here pass from Grenville to Carrillon, where you are.

"All aboard," as the conductor says; the bell on the engine rings, and you are on the high road to Grenville.

This road passes through farms in all stages of clearing—the numerous shanties betokening that they are held by their original proprietors, who are struggling to see them all cleared some day, and present a very different scene from what they do at present. Passing through, therefore—dismal enough swamp—some good land—farms cleared and uncleared—you arrive at Chatham Station (C. E). You will remember that you are now in Canada East—the other side of the River Ottawa, all the way up, nearly to its source, being Canada West; you, no doubt, are aware that Canada East is inhabited chiefly by French Canadians, (Roman Catholics,) and Canada West chiefly by British, or descendants of such, (and mostly Protestants,) the Scotch people forming a large portion of the population in Canada West. Passing Chatham Station—and a good many cleared farms in its neighborhood—you shortly reach Grenville, where the train stops, and you take the steamer "Phœnix." Here again look after your baggage, and see it on board.

At Grenville, you cannot fail to be forcibly struck with the beauty of the scenery now disclosed to your view. Not being of a poetical disposition, we regret our inability to do it that justice, in our description of it, to which it is entitled. From this point, the steamer turns round, to start on towards Ottawa, 58 miles off (6¼ hours). To our mind, this is the finest scene on the whole trip. The Ottawa here forms a sort of bay, with exquisitely beautiful scenery all round it—on one side a range of hills, stretching along as far as the eye can carry, wooded to their tops. The scenery reminds us of the vicinity of Ellen's Isle, on Loch Katrine, (Scot.,) only, that on the Ottawa, at this point, the hills are wooded—whilst those of the Scottish lake are barren—or covered only with pasture and heather.

Passing on from this charming point of view, the steamer now goes direct up the river for Ottawa City, making several stops by the way: the first is Hartwick's old landing, next, L'Original, with its excellent pier, and pretty, quiet little town in the distance.

Proceeding on, you will pass, on the right hand or north side of the river, the lands of the Papineau Seigniory, belonging to L. J. Papineau, of 1837 Canadian rebellion notoriety. This gentleman, we believe, still strongly adheres to his republican opinions, and is not a member in the Canadian legislature, at present. Before the rebellion alluded to, Mr. Papineau held the office of Speaker, and at the time of the rebellion, it is said government was due him about $4,000, which, on the restoration of peace, etc., he received on his return from exile, notwithstanding that he had been one of the leaders in that movement, in 1837.

The seigniory extends for abꞷut 15 miles, and is considered one of the poorest in Canada. As you pass on, you will observe the beautiful range of hills, to the north, which, from the different sizes and shapes they assume, present, with their shrubbery, a beautiful fringe work, to the scene all around. These hills form part of the chain, which range from Labrador, all the way to the Rocky Mountains.

Passing the stopping point of Montebello, you will observe Mr. Papineau's residence, embosomed amongst trees and shrubbery of beautiful foliage. It is called Papineau's Castle —Cape St. Marie. At this point, the steamer turns to the left, leaving the hills referred to, behind you. From Mr. Papineau's house, a most magnificent view of the river, and surrounding country, must be had—occupying so prominent a position, at the bend of the river, which there forms a sort of bay.

Proceeding on, you will now observe that the scenery assumes rather a different aspect, but still beautiful in its character. You sail past little islands wooded all over, and on between the banks of the river—which in some places become very flat, with the river extending in amongst the forest. At a more advanced season of the year, the river is lower, consequently, much of the water previously spread over a great portion of the country, recedes during the summer months, and before the winter season sets in, a heavy crop of hay is reaped. For nearly eight months in the year, however, the ground is thus covered with the swelling of the river, and of course only fit for cultivation during the hot season of about four months' duration.

You are now approaching to a place about twenty-eight miles of Ottawa—called Thurso —which presents nothing particular but an immense yard full of sawn lumber, belonging to the greatest lumbering establishment in the world—Pollok, Gilmour & Co., of Glasgow, (Scotland,) being one of the many stations which that firm have in Canada, for carrying on their immense trade. From off immense tracts of land, which they hold from government for a mere trifle—situated in different districts on the Ottawa—they have the lumber brought to wharves on the river, made into rafts and then floated down; that intended for the ports on the St. Lawrence and United States, to the west of Montreal, going via Lachine, whilst the greater proportion goes via the route you have been travelling—over the rapids and down to Lake St. Peter's, on the St. Lawrence, till it finally reaches Quebec. There it is sold or shipped by them to ports in Great Britain, large quantities of it finding its way to the Clyde (Scotland). Opposite to Thurso, will be observed what is called Foxe's Point. An English family of that name have settled there, and to this day they appear not to have forgot their taste for neat, well-trimmed grounds, fences, etc., exhibiting many of the characteristics of an Englishman's home. Passing on, you next stop at probably the wharf for Buckingham, (C. E.,) 17 miles inland. Opposite to this landing is Cumberland, (C. W.); passing which, you will shortly reach Gill's wharf, 6 miles from Ottawa, and the last stopping-place previous to reaching there.

In half an hour or so, you will observe the bluffs of Ottawa in the distance, but no appearance of the city, it being situated on ground high above the level of the river, where you land at. To the left you will notice the beautiful little waterfall of the Rideau—a Niagara in miniature—with its Goat Island between the horse shoe and straight line fall. It falls about 30 feet, and forms one of the prettiest little falls to be seen almost anywhere. On the right hand, you will observe a cluster of wooden shanties, at the mouth of the river Gatineau, which there joins the Ottawa, and, as you stand admiring the beauty of the scenery before, behind, and around you, the steamer touches at the wharf of Ottawa City. From the deck of the steamer, you will have an excellent view of the suspension bridge and the Chauderie Falls in the distance, with the rapids and the falls, throwing up the spray all around, forming a white cloud over the bridge. At the wharf you will find vehicles waiting to convey you to any hotel or address you may wish to go to. On reaching the top of the steep incline from the steamer, you will then obtain a first sight, perhaps, of Ottawa City, which was to have been the seat of the Canadian Government—and which may be yet—should the whim or interest of the members of the provincial parliament not decree otherwise.

The steamer "Lady Simpson," from Lachine to Grenville, is partly owned by its captain—Sheppard.

The steamer "Phœnix"—on board which you will find an excellent dinner for fifty cents, (2s. stg.,)—is commanded by a very civil and obliging Scotchman named McLachlan—who will be glad to point out to you the beauties of the river. From Grenville to Ottawa—a French-Canadian pilot takes charge of the steering of the vessel.

Parties who go to Ottawa City—by rail, via Prescott—as described elsewhere, can return *from* Ottawa by the route now described, and we have no doubt they will be pleased with one of the finest river trips we have experienced in America. The scenery of the Ottawa, just described, is by no means so bold in character as that of the noble river Hudson, from New York to Albany and Troy—still, it is one which cannot fail to afford the highest satisfaction to the tourist.

For bolder scenery, and the highlands of the Ottawa—see next page for account of the Upper Ottawa—being a continuation of the same river from Ottawa—away north-west —extending to parts as yet untrod by few, if any, white men—far less by tourists.

MONTREAL TO OTTAWA, C. W.

VIA GRAND TRUNK RAILROAD.

TAKE the cars on the Grand Trunk Railroad from station in Griffin Town, 1¼ miles from post-office, Montreal. Started from the station, you proceed, getting a fine view of the St. Lawrence on the left, the mountain on the right, and the fine landscape stretching beyond, till you reach Point Claire—15 miles. Leaving there, you proceed on through a beautiful country till you reach the magnificent bridge which crosses the river Ottawa at St. Anne's, going over which you get a hasty glance of the Ottawa stretching far beyond to the west, assuming the appearance of a magnificent lake, situated in a basin, surrounded by finely-wooded hills in the background, and richly-wooded country on every side of it. Immediately under this bridge you may observe the rapids rushing along, and also the locks where the steamer for the Ottawa River, from Lachine, passes through to avoid these —called "St. Anne's rapids"—from the name of the village close by.

You pass on to Vaudreuil, 24 miles; Cedars, 29 miles; Coteau Landing, 37 miles; River Beaudette, 44 miles; Lancaster, 54 miles; Summerstown, 60 miles; Cornwall, 68 miles; Moulinette, 73 miles; Dickinson Landing, 77 miles; Aultsville, 84 miles; Williamsburg, 92 miles; Matilda, 99 miles; Edwardsburg, 104 miles, to Prescott Junction, 112 miles from Montreal.

At Prescott Junction, you change cars, and take those on the line from Prescott to Ottawa, 54 miles distant, stopping at eight stations between these points. The stranger, if newly arrived, either via Quebec, or New York, from Great Britain, or continent of Europe, will, on this line, get the first glimpse, most likely, of "bush life," of "shanties," and "cleared," or "partially cleared" lands. The line being a succession of dense forest, swamp, and partially cleared farms, presents few or no interesting features to the tourist farther than those mentioned. Between the last station (Gloucester) and Ottawa (11 miles off) the country presents a much more cleared appearance, and a few well-cultivated farms will be seen along the line of railroad, until it arrives at the station, close to New Edinburgh, on the one side of the Rideau River, with Ottawa on the other side, about a quarter of a mile off.

You will find vehicles in waiting, which will convey yourself and luggage to whatever hotel you please. Campbell's Hotel, Ottawa, we can recommend.

For description of Ottawa, see elsewhere.

After you have visited Ottawa, its river above the town, etc., etc., you can return to Montreal, via steamer on the River Ottawa, via Grenville, Lachine, etc., (see **Montreal to Ottawa, via Lachine and steamer,**) or the way you came.

UNITED STATES TO OTTAWA, C. W.

PRESCOTT JUNCTION, on the Grand Trunk Railway, 112 miles from Montreal, is the nearest point for tourists and emigrants from the United States.

Prescott is approached by steamer from Ogdensburg, opposite side of the river.

Or via rail to Cape Vincent, thence steamer to Kingston, and rail to Prescott.

Or via steamer all the way, viz., Cape Vincent, passing through the Thousand Islands, past Brockville on to Prescott.

Or via steamer to Brockville, thence rail to Prescott Junction.

From Prescott to Ottawa proceed per rail, as mentioned in preceding route. See "Montreal to Ottawa," per Grand Trunk Railroad.

From Suspension Bridge or Niagara Falls, per Great Western Rail to Toronto, and thence Grand Trunk Railroad to Prescott Junction; thence, rail. Or steamer from Lewiston or Niagara to Toronto, and thence steamer on Canada side, or by the American line of steamers from Lewiston and Niagara direct to Brockville or Ogdensburg.

THE UPPER RIVER OTTAWA.

A DESCRIPTION of the lower portion of the Ottawa we have given elsewhere, in a trip from Montreal to Ottawa, leaving the river on reaching the town of Ottawa.

For an authentic description of the upper portion of this wonderful river, we annex particulars regarding it, from a report made to the House of Assembly, some time ago. The description of the river which follows, commences *at the source* of the river, and proceeds on *towards Ottawa*, till it reaches the point we left off at:

The length of the course of the Ottawa River is about 780 miles. From its source it bends in a south-west course, and after receiving several tributaries from the height of land separating its waters from the Hudson's Bay, it enters Lake Temiscaming. From its entrance into this lake downward the course of the Ottawa has been surveyed, and is well known.

At the head of the lake the Blanch River falls in, coming about 90 miles from the north. Thirty-four miles farther down the lake it receives the Montreal River, coming 120 miles from the north-west. Six miles lower down on the east, or Lower Canada bank, it receives the Keepawasippi, a large river, which has its origin in a lake of great size, hitherto but partially explored, and known as Lake Keepawa. This lake is connected with another chain of irregularly-shaped lakes, from one of which proceeds the River du Moine, which enters the Ottawa about 100 miles below the mouth of the Keepawasippi, the double discharge from the same chain of lakes in opposite directions, presents a phenomenon similar to the connection between the Orinoco and Rio Negro in South America.

From the Long Sault at the foot of Lake Temiscaming, 233 miles above Bytown, and 360 miles from the mouth of the Ottawa, down to Deux Joachim Rapids, at the head of the Deep River, that is for 89 miles, the Ottawa, with the exception of 17 miles below the Long Sault, and some other intervals, is not at present navigable, except for canoes. Besides other tributaries in the interval, at 197 miles from Ottawa, it receives on the west side the Mattawan, which is the highway for canoes going to Lake Huron, by Lake Nipissing. From the Mattawan the Ottawa flows east by south to the head of Deep River Reach, 9 miles above which it receives the River Du Moine from the north.

From the head of Deep River—as this part of the Ottawa is called—to the foot of Upper Allumette Lake, 2 miles below the village of Pembroke, is an uninterrupted reach of navigable water, 43 miles in length. The general direction of the river, in this part, is south-east. The mountains along the north side of Deep River are upwards of 1000 *feet in height*, and the many wooded islands of Allumette Lake render the scenery of this part of the Ottawa magnificent and picturesque—even said to surpass the celebrated Lake of the Thousand Islands on the St. Lawrence.

Passing the short rapid of Allumettes, and turning northward, round the lower end of Allumettes Island, which is 14 miles long, and 8 at its greatest width, and turning down south-east through Coulonge Lake, and passing behind the nearly similar Islands of Calumet, to the head of the Calumet Falls, the Ottawa presents, with the exception of one slight rapid, a reach of 50 miles of navigable water. The mountains on the north side of Coulonge Lake, which rise apparently to the height of 1500 feet, add a degree of grandeur to the scenery, which is, in other respects, beautiful and varied. In the Upper Allumettes Lake, 1500 miles from Ottawa, the river receives from the west the Petawawee, one of its largest tributaries. This river is 140 miles in length, and drains an area of 2,200 square miles. At Pembroke, 9 miles lower down on the same side, an inferior stream, the Indian River, also empties itself into the Ottawa.

At the head of Lake Coulonge, the Ottawa receives from the north the Black River, 130 miles in length, draining an area of 1120 miles; and 9 miles lower, on the same side, the River Coulonge, which is probably 160 miles in length, with a valley of 1800 square miles.

From the head of the Calumet Falls, to Portage du Fort, the head of the steamboat navigation, a distance of 80 miles, are impassable rapids. Fifty miles above the city the Ottawa receives on the west the Bonechere, 110 miles in length, draining an area of 980 miles. Eleven miles lower, it receives the Madawaska, one of its greatest feeders, a river 210 miles in length, and draining 4,100 square miles.

Thirty-seven miles above Ottawa, there is an interruption in the navigation, caused by 3 miles of rapids and falls, to pass which a railroad has been made. At the foot of the rapids, the Ottawa divides among islands.

Six miles above Ottawa begins the rapids, terminating in the Chaudière Falls, Ottawa. The greatest height of the Chaudière Falls is about 40 feet.

TRIP TO THE RIVER SAGUENAY.

For about $12, a trip can be enjoyed to and from one of the most magnificent districts in Canada—where nature appears in all her wild and secluded grandeur.

Tourists take the steamer from Quebec, which sails generally every Wednesday.

To quote from one who visited this district, "You leave in the morning, and passing down the St. Lawrence, put in at several places for passengers, which gives an opportunity of seeing the *habitans*, and the old-fashioned French settlements of St. Thomas, River Ouelle, Kamouraska, and many others, together with Orleans Island, Crane Island, Goose Island, and the Pilgrims. The north and south shores of the river are thickly studded with parish churches, having spires of tin which glitter in the sun like shining silver ; these, and the whitewashed farm-houses, form two objects characteristic of Lower Canada. By sunset you arrive at River du Loup. The water is quite salt, and the river, expanding to the breadth of 20 miles, gives it the appearance of an open sea ; and it is much frequented as a sea-bathing place.

" Here you remain all night on board, so as to be ready for an early start at dawn, when you stretch across for the north shore, steering for a great gap in the mountains. This is the mouth of the Saguenay, one of the most singular rivers in the world; not a common river, with undulating banks and shelving shores, and populous villages: not a river precipitous on one side, and rolling land on the other, formed by the washing away of the mountains for ages: this is not a river of that description. It is perfectly straight, with a sheer precipice on each side, without any windings, or projecting bluffs, or sloping banks, or sandy shores. It is as if the mountain range had been cleft asunder, leaving a horrid gulf of 60 miles in length, and 4000 feet in depth, through the grey mica-schist, and still looking new and fresh. 1500 feet of this is perpendicular cliff, often too steep and solid for the hemlock or dwarf oak to find root ; in which case, being covered with coloured lichens and moss, these fresh-looking fractures often look, in shape and colour, like painted fans, and are called the Pictured Rocks. But those parts, more slanting, are thickly covered with stunted trees, spruce and maple, and birch, growing wherever they can find crevices to extract nourishment: and the bare roots of the oak, grasping the rock, have a resemblance to gigantic claws. The base of these cliffs lie far under water, to an unknown depth. For many miles from its mouth, no soundings have been obtained with 2000 feet of line, and for the entire distance of 60 miles, until you reach Ha-ha Bay, the largest ships can sail without obstruction from banks or shoals, and on reaching the extremity of the bay, can drop their anchor in 30 fathoms.

"The view up this river is singular in many respects; hour after hour, as you sail along, precipice after precipice unfolds itself to view, as in a moving panorama, and you sometimes forget the size and height of the objects you are contemplating, until reminded by seeing a ship of 1000 tons lying like a small pinnace under the towering cliff to which she is moored; for, even in these remote and desolate regions, industry is at work, and, although you cannot much discern it, saw-mills have been built on some of the tributary streams which fall into the Saguenay. But what strikes one most, is the absence of beach or strand; for except in a few places where mountain torrents, rushing through gloomy ravines, have washed down the detritus of the hills, and formed some alluvial land at the mouth, no coves, nor creeks, nor projecting rocks are seen in which a boat could find shelter, or any footing be obtained. The characteristic is a steep wall of rock, rising abruptly from the water—a dark and desolate region, where all is cold and gloomy; the mountains hidden with driving mist, the water black as ink, and cold as ice. No ducks nor sea-gulls sitting on the water, or screaming for their prey; no hawks nor eagles soaring overhead, although there is abundance of what might be called Eagle Cliffs;' no deer coming down to drink at the streams; no squirrels nor birds to be seen among the trees; no fly on the water, nor swallow skimming over the surface. It reminds you of

'That lake whose gloomy shore
Sky-lark never warbled o'er.'

One living thing you may see, but it is a cold-blooded animal; you may see the cold seal, spreading himself upon his clammy rock, watching for his prey. And this is all you see for the first 20 miles, save the ancient settlement of Tadousac at the entrance, and the pretty cove of L'Ance a l'Eau, which is a fishing station.

"Now you reach Cape Eternité, Cape Trinité, and many other overhanging cliffs, remarkable for having such clean fractures, seldom equalled for boldness and effect, which create constant apprehensions of danger, even in a calm; but if you happen to be caught in a thunder-storm, the roar, and darkness, and flashes of lightning are perfectly appalling. At last you terminate your voyage at Ha-ha Bay, that is, smiling or laughing bay in the Indian language, for you are perfectly charmed and relieved to arrive at a beautiful spot where you have sloping banks, a pebbly shore, boats and wherries, and vessels riding at anchor, birds and animals, a village, a church, French Canadians and Scottish Highlanders, and in short, there is nothing can remind one more of a scene in Argyleshire.

"The day is now half spent; you have been ashore, looking through the village, examining into the nature of what appears a very thriving settlement; the inhabitants seem to be all French and Scotch, understanding each other's language, and living in perfect amity. You hear that Mr. Price, of Quebec, is the gentlemen to whom all this improvement is due. That it is he who has opened up the Saguenay country, having erected many saw-mills, each the nucleus of a village, and that a trade in sawed lumber is carried on to the extent of 100 ship loads in the season. The river is navigable for ships as far as Chicoutimi, about 70 miles from its mouth. An extensive lumbering establishment is there, and the timber is collected in winter through all the neighbouring country, as far as Lake St. John, which is 50 miles further up, and is the grand source of the Saguenay.

"After having seen and heard all this, you get on board, weigh anchor, pass again down the river, reviewing the solemn scene, probably meeting neither vessel, boat nor canoe, through all the dreary way, and arrive at the mouth of the river in time to cross to River du Loup, where you again find a safe harbour for the night. Next day you again pass up the St. Lawrence, stopping for a short time at Murray Bay, a beautiful grassy valley on the north shore, surrounded by wooded mountains, and much frequented by Quebec families, as a bathing place. You arrive at Quebec in the evening, thus taking just 3 days for your excursion, at an expense of about $12."

FALLS OF MONTMORENCI, NEAR QUEBEC.

Few strangers visit Quebec without going to see the Falls of Montmorenci. These Falls, which are situated in a beautiful nook of the river, are higher than those of Niagara, being more than two hundred and fifty feet; but they are very narrow, being only some fifty feet wide. This place is a very celebrated focus of winter amusements. During the frost, the spray from the Falls accumulates to such an extent as to form a cone of some eighty feet high. There is also a second cone of inferior altitude, and it is this of which visitors make the most use, as being less dangerous than the higher one. They carry "toboggins,"—long, thin pieces of wood—and having arrived at the summit, place themselves on these and slide down with immense velocity. Ladies and gentlemen both enter with equal spirit into this amusement. It requires much skill to avoid accidents; but sometimes people do tumble heels over head to the bottom. They generally drive to this spot in sleighs, taking their wine and provisions with them; and upon the pure white cloth which nature has spread out for them, they partake of their dainty repast and enjoy a most agreeable pic-nic. One does not feel in the least cold, as the exercise so thoroughly warms and invigorates the system. The distance of these Falls from Quebec is eight miles.

OTTAWA, CANADA WEST.

The notoriety which this city, in embryo, has received lately, first as being fixed upon as the seat of government for Canada, and then decided against as such by the provincial legislature,—although it had been acquiesced in by Her Majesty as the most advisable locality—has invested it with a significance which, otherwise, it would not, in all probability, have obtained.

Ottawa is the new name given to the town of Bytown, by which it has long been known, as the centre of the immense lumber district of the River Ottawa. It is situated on that river, where the Rivers Ridea and Gatineau, and the Rideau Canal, all meet.

The town is intersected by the Rideau Canal and bridge, and forms three districts, viz.: that of Lower Town, on the east; Central Town, on the west; and Upper Town, on the north-west; all of which, however, are on the south side of the River Ottawa, and in Canada West, the River Ottawa, as is well known, forming the boundary line between Canada East and Canada West. The town was laid out under the command of Colonel By of the Royal Engineers, who constructed, also, the Rideau Canal. Hence the original name of the town being called Bytown—although now called Ottawa, after the magnificent river on which it stands.

The streets are all wide and regularly laid out, and, so far, reflects great credit on the engineering skill employed. Lower Town is the most important portion of the town, and, in all probability, will become the chief business part, as the population and business increases. The two principal streets of Lower Town are Rideau street and Sussex street. In Rideau street there are several substantial, stone-built stores and dwellings. In Sussex street there are also a few; the majority, however, are wooden erections, both old and new. In Central Town the buildings are almost all of stone, presenting one excellent street, called Spark street; whilst Upper Town exhibits a mixture of both stone and wooden buildings in its Wellington street. All the buildings in the town are exceedingly plain, but substantially built, and, being built of gray limestone, resemble very much in appearance some of the streets of Montreal, as well as in the granite city of Aberdeen (Scotland). On "Barrack Hill," the highest elevation of the town, are situated what are termed the government buildings—the remains, however, we should say, rather than of actual buildings. There are a few small out-houses and offices—which certainly do not deserve the name of government buildings—with sundry small cannon, taking their ease on the ground alongside of carriages, which have evidently seen service of some sort. These are the "dogs of war," which are intended, we presume, to protect the town against all invaders. On Barrack Hill is, however, also the residence of the chief military authority of the place. The "location" of these buildings and the "gun battery" alluded to, is certainly one of the finest we have seen any where, either in Canada or the United States—equal, in some respects, even to the famous citadel of Quebec. In the rear is Central Town, whilst Upper and Lower Town are completely commanded by it on each side, whilst in front is a precipitous embankment running down, almost perpendicular, to the river, several hundred feet, thus completely sweeping the river and opposite shore, north, east, and west; so that, in a military point of view, Ottawa certainly occupies one of the finest natural positions any where in Canada; and, in that respect, is the key to an immense territory of back country, valuable for its wood and minerals.

The stranger, on visiting Ottawa for the first time, is apt to be disappointed that he does not find a larger "city," and one more advanced, in many respects; but it must be recollected that it has been forced into public notice from the cause we have already alluded to, and obtained a publicity with which parties at a distance are apt to connect wrong or exaggerated ideas; and if the town is not larger than it is, the fault rests as much in the imaginations of individuals, as with the inhabitants, generally, of the town itself, who, in the short time, since Bytown became a place of note, have been doing their utmost to make it "go a-head." In the desire to do so, however, some of the landholders there, we fear, by putting very high prices on their lots, and landlords refusing to give

OTTAWA, CANADA WEST. — LOWER, AND PART OF CENTRAL, TOWN.

OTTAWA, CANADA WEST.—UPPER TOWN, LOOKING WEST.

leases at reasonable rates, have only tended to defeat the very object which they, and all the inhabitants ought to have in view, viz., giving every facility in their power, and offering every inducement they can, for parties at a distance to locate amongst them. In fact, the idea that Ottawa was selected as the headquarters of the government, has had any thing but a beneficial effect so far, in some respects, upon the town; but there is the consolation, that whether it is to be the seat of government or not, there is no doubt, that of necessity, it is destined to become—it may be gradually—the centre of a much more extensive trade, a town of much greater importance than it is at present, and the point, round which radiate a number of other towns, and extensive agricultural districts, of which Ottawa is the capital and centre, and, in all human probability, always likely to remain so. From it, a large wholesale and retail trade is, and must always, be done—with the districts round about; whilst, as is well known, it is the centre of a district, which, for extensive forests of fine lumber, has no superior in America.

The scenery around Ottawa is far beyond what we had any idea of, and the view from the Barrack Hill, is one of surpassing grandeur and extent, combining in it a trinity of river, landscape, and fall scenery, which few places can boast of.

Looking to the west—(see engraving)—at the west end of the town are situated, the celebrated Chaudiere Falls, which fall about 40 feet, and the spray of which may be seen a long way off, ascending in the air.

In the early part of the season, (say in May,) these falls are not seen to so much advantage, the river then being, generally, so much swollen with the immense volume of water from the upper lakes and the tributaries of the Ottawa. Then they partake, in some respects, more of the character of huge rapids. Farther on in the season, however, they appear more in their real character of "falls," and are a sight worth seeing, although they are being very much encroached upon, by lumber establishments. An excellent view of the falls, as well as of the rapids, is got from off the suspension bridge, which crosses the river quite close to them. At the eastern suburb of Ottawa, again, called New Edinburgh, there is a little Niagara, in miniature, in the Rideau Falls, and one of the prettiest little falls to be seen any where. Although only of 30 feet fall, they present features of interest and great beauty.

The town of Ottawa is supplied, in many parts, with gas. Its markets afford an excellent supply of cheap provisions, whilst the purity of the air, from its elevated position, renders it one of the healthiest towns in Canada.

Emigrants, in looking to Ottawa, will do well to remember, that it is only the agricultural labourer, or farmer with capital, to whom its locality offers inducements at present.

Amongst the schemes for connecting Canada East with the Western States, is the Ottawa Ship Canal, via the Ottawa and French Rivers to Lake Huron, which, if successful in being established, will render Ottawa, more than ever, one of the great entrepots of that route and traffic.

The communication between Ottawa and Montreal, is by rail via Prescott; also by river, per steamer to Grenville, rail from Grenville to Carrillon; thence, steamer to Lachine; thence, rail to Montreal. To Canada West, on the St. Lawrence, via rail. To Ogdensburg, via rail to Prescott, and steamer across the St. Lawrence. Distances:—from Montreal, 126 miles; Quebec, 296 miles; Toronto, 223 miles; Kingston, 95 miles; Prescott, 55 miles; New York, 450 miles; Boston, 485 miles. Population, about 12,000.

THE Rideau Canal extends from Ottawa to Kingston, and was constructed entirely at the expense of the British government. It was commenced in September, 1826, and the first steamboat passed through it in May, 1832. Length of the canal from Ottawa to Kingston, 126¼ miles. Actual excavation, 16¼ miles.

THE LOCKS ON THE RIDEAU CANAL, OTTAWA, C. W.,

SHOWING THE WATER CONNECTION BETWEEN THAT CANAL AND RIVER OTTAWA.

Number of locks ascending from Ottawa to the isthmus, 87½ miles, and overcoming a rise of 292 feet—34 locks. Number of locks descending from the isthmus to Kingston, 38¾ miles, descent 165 feet—13 locks. Length of locks, 134 feet. Breadth of locks, 33 feet. Depth of water in canal, 5 feet. Breadth of the surface of canal, 75 feet.

The bridge seen in the upper portion of the engraving, is the one which connects Lower Town with Upper and Central Town, Ottawa. The masonry of which these locks are composed, is of the most massive character, and, altogether, they have been built regardless of expense.

Total cost of construction, $2,890,000, (£772,000)(?)

62

CITY OF TORONTO, C W.

Toronto forms the Metropolis of Upper Canada, (or Canada West,) the second city in commercial importance in the entire province, and at present is the seat of the provincial legislature. It is pleasantly situated on the west shore of Lake Ontario, and has a much more prepossessing appearance when viewed from a steamer on the lake, than when approached by railway. From the large quantity of trees and shrubbery interspersed through many of the streets, it may well lay claim to the title of the Forest City of Canada. Situated as the city is, on almost a dead level, it presents no particular features further than being plentifully studded with graceful spires, which, with the wooded hills situated in the background, completes the picture of a beautiful city.

The street along side of the shore of the lake—recently very much improved—is termed the Esplanade, along which the Grand Trunk Railroad runs, and where it has its terminus.

CROWN-LANDS' OFFICE AND MECHANICS' INSTITUTE.

ST. LAWRENCE HALL.

In one portion of the above building are the offices of the Crown-land Department, where all business connected with the "Woods and Forests" are conducted In another portion is the excellent Mechanics' Institution of the city, situated at the corner of Church and Adelaide streets.

The above forms one of the most imposing buildings in the city. The basement and first floors are occupied as stores, whilst upstairs there is a large, well-lighted, and neatly done-up public hall, where meetings, concerts, etc., are held. St. Lawrence Hall is situated at the east end of King street.

KING STREET (WEST).

YONGE STREET (NORTH).

King street is the principal thoroughfare in the city. It is fully 2 miles in length, and with its many handsome stores and buildings, forms the chief promenade. Two of the largest buildings in the city are in King street, viz., St. Lawrence Hall, and the Rossin House.

Yonge street rivals King street, in its busy bustling appearance, and although the stores are not so elegant as some in King street, yet a large amount of retail business is transacted in the section presented above.

As in most cities in the United States, the streets of Toronto are long and spacious, and laid out at right angles to each other.

The principal streets for wholesale stores are the lower end of Yonge street and Wellington street, whilst Upper Yonge street and King street are the chief streets for retail business of all sorts.

We may mention that, with the exception of spaces here and there, the pavements in all the streets are of wood—planks laid across, and nailed down to sleepers.

The Provincial Legislature holds its meetings in Toronto, in the government buildings, a cluster of red brick buildings situated at the west end of the city, close to which is the residence of the Governor-General, Sir Edmund Walker Head, Bart., representative of Her Majesty in Canada.

The public buildings of Toronto are numerous, and some of them very handsome. We have engraved, from photographs, four of the principal buildings, viz.: St. Lawrence Hall, Trinity College, the Normal School, and Crown-lands Office, in which building is also situated the Mechanics' Institute. Osgoode Hall, in Queen street, when completed will form one of the finest buildings in the city. There the Superior Courts of Law and Equity are held. Besides those named, the other public buildings of any note are the Post-office, the new General Hospital and the Lunatic Asylum—the latter an immense building at the western extremity of the city.

Toronto may well boast as being the city of churches in Canada, from the number of elegant structures it contains, of all denominations. The two largest are the English Cathedral and the Roman Catholic Cathedral, but both, being without spires as yet, do not present that graceful appearance which even some of the smaller churches do, although none, we should suppose, exceed the rich and handsome interior or comfortable accommodation of the English Cathedral, as a place of worship.

Toronto has several manufacturing establishments, some of them extensive, and which, in ordinary good times, turn over a large amount of business; the city, from its central position, and the ready means of land and water carriage, now extended almost in every direction, affording great facilities for manufactures as well as merchandise finding their way all over the country.

TRINITY COLLEGE.

THE NORMAL AND MODEL SCHOOLS.

The above building is one of the most important in the city, whether as regards its character as an educational institution, or the magnificent style of the edifice, which, when completed, will certainly be one of the finest in the city.

The above building, in the Italian style of architecture, is devoted to the establishment known as the Normal and Model Schools, and which forms the head of that invaluable system of public education pervading the whole province.

As we have said, Toronto forms the second commercial city in Canada, and, until the panic of 1857 set in, enjoyed a large and steadily increasing trade. Its merchants were of the most enterprising, active, and "go a-head" character; consequently probably no city in America has experienced the effects of the panic more than Toronto. With the general revival of business, we have no doubt, it will assume its wonted activity, although it may be gradually.

The railways centring in Toronto are:—The Great Western, to Hamilton; Suspension Bridge, (Niagara,) and Windsor, opposite Detroit, (Michigan).

The Grand Trunk, to Montreal and Quebec, (east,) and to Stratford, (west).

The Ontario, Simcoe, and Huron, (now called the Northern Railroad,) to Collingwood.

THE UNIVERSITY, TORONTO, C. W.

THE foundation-stone of this magnificent building was laid in 1857, and it is expected to be available for the University classes at the commencement of the academic year of 1859-60. When completed, it will undoubtedly justify the eulogistic remarks of the editor of the Toronto "Globe," who says:—"It will be, without question, the finest structure in Canada, and, we believe, the most imposing one devoted to educational purposes, on the whole continent."

In 1827, a charter was granted, by George the Fourth, for the establishment of a University at York, (now Toronto,) to be designated "King's College;" and, in the following year, the institution was endowed with a portion of the "Lands" which had been previously set apart, for educational purposes, by George the Third. It was not, however, until 1857, that decisive steps were taken to commence the work of building. On the 22d of February, of that year, the Governor-General authorized the Senate of the University to erect suitable buildings, at an expense not to exceed $75,000, (£15,000 sterling) to be drawn from the University Fund. In addition, the sum of $20,000 (£4,000 sterling) was granted for the purchase of a library and museum.

The general outline of the buildings approaches the form of a square, having an internal quadrangle of about 200 feet, the north side of which opens on the Park. The south front is 300 feet long, having a massive Norman tower in the centre, 100 feet in height, surmounted by four pinnacles, each 30 feet high. The east side is 260 feet, and the west side about 200 feet in length.

The general accommodation is comprised in the lecture, theatre and nine class-rooms, with professors' rooms attached; library and reading rooms, museum, with preparation and curator's rooms; senate chamber, chancellor's rooms and other University offices; the convocation hall, president's and dean's residences; quarters for 60 students, with college dining-hall and all necessary appurtenances.

THE UNIVERSITY, TORONTO.

CITY OF KINGSTON, C. W.

The City of Kingston is one of the most delightfully situated places in Canada. It is midway between Montreal and Toronto, at the foot of Lake Ontario, and at the head of the River St. Lawrence, whose fairy-like Architecture Archipelago of a Thousand Isles has given it a celebrity little less than world-wide. On approaching the city, the view, both from lake and river, is very fine, and impresses the traveller with a most favourable idea of it. For solidity, Kingston will compare favourably with any city on the continent; being built on, and surrounded by immense beds of limestone—this material, besides being a source of revenue, is also generally used in the construction of its buildings, varied of late years, and interspersed here and there, with three and four story brick, with a fair proportion of frame, structures, making the contrast particularly-striking. Its chief attraction, as well as ornament, is the immense "City Hall Buildings," fronting on Ontario street, than which there is not a more imposing pile in all Canada. It is a handsome cut stone edifice, in the shape of the letter T—the front elevation being in chaste Palladian style, the centre of which is surmounted with a dome, commanding a fine prospect of the city and the bay, and from which a good view of the surrounding country is obtained. These buildings, besides the immense Hall, which is used on all public occasions, and for concerts, etc., contain the common council chambers, city offices, commercial news room, agency of the bank of British North America, temporary post-office, wholesale stores and warehouses, together with numerous other offices, etc., which will give some idea of its proportions. Its average cost was one hundred and twenty thousand dollars. The new "Court House and Jail," now completed, stands next in order, and is, indeed, an ornament to the city, the front elevation, with its six magnificent pillars, being in Grecian Ionic style, and the design extremely chaste and elegant. Its length is 208 feet, width 54 feet. The average outlay in its construction was nearly ninety thousand dollars. The lower story is designed for public offices, above which are the court and council rooms, consisting of the assizes and county court, the division court, and county council rooms, etc. In rear are the Jail and jailer's dwelling, forming an extensive wing to the main building. The other buildings of note are, the Roman Catholic Cathedral, and Regiopolis College; the General Hospital, Queen's College, the Grammar School; St. George's, St. Paul's, and St. James's Protestant Churches; St. Andrew's Church, Irish Free Church, Chalmer's Church, Wesleyan and Primitive Methodist Churches, Congregational Church, Baptist Church, Apostolic Church, and the old French Roman Catholic Church, now used as a nunnery. The new Custom House and Post-office, recently completed, would be an ornament to any city. The chief public institutions are, the General Hospital, House of Industry, Hotel Dieu, Mechanics' Institute, etc. There are two daily newspapers—"The British Whig," the first daily published in Canada West, and "The News;" one tri-weekly in the Roman Catholic interest, the "Herald;" and four weeklies, the "Chronicle and News," the "British Whig," the "Commercial Advertiser," and the "Tribune." One thing must not be overlooked in mentioning the lions of the city—the Public Park, which, in a few years, will be a chief source of healthful recreation to the citizens.

Kingston has long been known for its safe and capacious harbour, which is well adapted to shelter a large fleet of vessels, besides having over twenty wharves, some of them very extensive, and furnished with capacious warehouses and accommodations for the forwarding trade. The shipping trade has long been a chief feature of the place. In addition to the ship yards at Garden Island, opposite, and at Portsmouth, at the extreme west end of the city, there is the noted Marine Railway of John Counter, Esq., from all of which have been launched the greatest number and largest tonnage of Canadian vessels in Canada West. Kingston, in this particular, being only second to Quebec.

A branch railroad has lately been made across a portion of the bay below the Cataraqui Bridge, to connect with the city from the main depot, coming in at the foot of Ontario street, at the Téte du Pont barracks, and passing thence along the harbour to Shaw's wharf, where the branch or city depot is to be established. Kingston has, also, her Crystal Palace, at the outskirts of the city, in which the County Agricultural, Horticultural, and other shows are held, and in which will be held the Provincial Association's great Annual Show for 1859. This is a large, handsome, and commodious building, which speaks favourably for the public enterprise of the Kingstonese, and the yeomenry of the county of Frontenac. Not the least remarkable evidence of the prosperity of the farming community, is the large markets in Kingston—larger, perhaps, than any others in Canada, and attesting greatly in favour of the superiority of the land in the vicinity.

Kingston is well defended, judging from her martello towers, market battery, and extensive and commanding fortifications at Fort Henry and Point Frederick. Towards the west end of the city are numerous handsome private residences, fronting on Lake Ontario. Still further on is the private Insane Asylum, at "Rockwood." The Penitentiary, situated on the lake shore, is a great attraction to strangers visiting Kingston. It is surrounded with walls 30 feet high, with flanking towers, the whole covering an area of about twenty acres. Inside the walls, the first building seen is of a cruciform shape, in one wing of which is the hospital; in another, the dining-hall; above these, the chapel; and underneath, the asylum for the insane. The north part is the dwelling-house of the Warden and other officers, with a beautiful garden attached; the remainder being occupied as cells for the convicts, who are all well cared for, and have, with their own hands, erected the walls, workshops, sheds, cells, etc. At the back, and next the lake side, are ranges of workshops, where the surplus labour is let to contractors.

On the whole, Kingston seems to keep the even tenour of her way amongst the cities of Canada West, with a creditable steadiness and perseverance; is said to be one of the most healthy localities in the province; with a population of about 13,000. Kingston is represented in the Upper House by the Honourable Alexander Campbell, and in the Lower House by the Honourable John A. Macdonald, the ex-Premier; the member for the county being the Honorable Henry Smith, Speaker of the Legislative Assembly.

The station of the Grand Trunk Railroad is about 2 miles from the city. Omnibuses ply to and from it, in connection with the hotels.

CITY OF HAMILTON, CANADA WEST.—From the Mountain.

LONDON, CANADA WEST.

Like its namesake, the great Babylon of England, London, C. W., is in the County of Middlesex, and also on the River Thames, with streets and bridges named after those of the great city. There, however, the similarity ends. It possesses some excellent public buildings and churches, and is situated in the centre of an extensive and rich agricultural district, which furnishes it with a large amount of trade in grain and other agricultural produce. Previous to the late commercial panic, few places showed greater signs of progress than London; in fact it went ahead too fast, like many other cities and towns, consequently it has felt the revulsion all the more—and every department of business, nearly, has suffered—to revive again, we hope, when business becomes more buoyant generally. The town is lighted with gas, and supports as many as six newspapers, and five bank agencies. The streets are wide, and laid off at right angles. London is one of the principal stations on the Great Western Railroad of Canada, on the section from Hamilton to Windsor, with a branch to port Stanley, on Lake Erie, from which there is a regular steam communication with Cleveland, Ohio.

The soil in the immediate vicinity of London, it is true, is sandy, and the country almost a dead level, as far as Windsor; but you cannot travel many miles in a northern or southern direction, until you meet with an undulating country, and productive farms, whose proprietors, of course, betake themselves to London for sale and purchase—for mart and market.

Our representation of London is from one of several photographs, supplied to us by Mr. E. H. Longman, of London, C. W., and, from the excellent manner in which they are executed, we feel pleasure and confidence in saying, that the photographic art is well represented there by Mr Longman—judging from the specimens he has supplied to us.

HAMILTON, C. W.

Hamilton, one of the cities of Canada West, is situated at the south-western extremity of Burlington Bay, an inlet at the head of Lake Ontario, and terminus of lake navigation. The site on which Hamilton is built, occupies gradually rising ground for about a mile and a half from the shore of the lake to the base of the hill, called the Mountain, which rises up in the background. It was laid out in 1813, and has spread with wonderful rapidity—faster than almost any other town in Canada. In 1841 the population was only about 3500, while in 1850 it had increased to 10,312, and now has reached to nearly 30,000.

Hamilton is the centre of one of the most extensive and best agricultural portions of Canada, and in its vicinity are to be seen some of the best cultivated farms, not long reclaimed from the primeval forest.

As in most American cities, the streets are laid out at right angles, and present a fine, spacious appearance. The public buildings, banks, churches and hotels, which are amongst the finest in the province, are built of stone and brick. Some of the merchants' stores excel any thing of the same sort in Toronto, or even Montreal, and are carried on by some of the largest importers in Canada, who do an extensive business throughout the country.

The chief business streets—named King, John, James, York, and McNab streets—are situated a considerable distance back from the shore.

The Gore Bank of Canada has its head-quarters in Hamilton, in addition to which there are five or six other Bank agencies.

The finest and certainly most extensive view of the city is to be had from the Mountain.

70

LONDON, CANADA WEST.

COMPARATIVE
TIME INDICATOR.